DOCUMENT 1

DOCUMENT 1

Book*hug
Toronto, 2018
Literature in Translation Series

FIRST ENGLISH EDITION

Published originally under the title *Document 1* © Les éditions de L'instant même, 2012
English translation copyright © 2018 by J.C. Sutcliffe

The production of this book was made possible through the generous assistance
of the Canada Council for the Arts and the Ontario Arts Council. Book*hug also acknowledges
the support of the Government of Canada through the Canada Book Fund and the Government
of Ontario through the Ontario Book Publishing Tax Credit and the Ontario Book Fund.

We acknowledge the financial support of the Government of Canada through the National
Translation Program for Book Publishing, an initiative of the *Roadmap for Canada's Official
Languages 2013-2018: Education, Immigration, Communities*, for our translation activites.

Book*hug acknowledges the land on which it operates. For thousands of years it has been
the traditional land of the Huron-Wendat, the Seneca, and most recently, the Mississaugas
of the Credit River. Today, this meeting place is still the home to many Indigenous people
from across Turtle Island, and we are grateful to have the opportunity to work on this land.

Library and Archives Canada Cataloguing in Publication

Blais, François, 1973– [Document 1. English]   Document 1 / François Blais ;
[translated by] J.C. Sutcliffe. —First English edition.

(Literature in translation series) Translation of: Document 1.
Issued in print and electronic formats.
ISBN 978-1-77166-378-6 (softcover)
ISBN 978-1-77166-379-3 (HTML)
ISBN 978-1-77166-380-9 (PDF)
ISBN 978-1-77166-381-6 (Kindle)

I. Sutcliffe, J. C., [date]–, translator II. Title. III. Title: Document one. IV. Series:
Literature in translation series

PS8603.L3282D6213 2018   C843'.6   C2018-900812-1
                                         C2018-900813-X

PRINTED IN CANADA

Sheer experience had already taught
her that, in some circumstances,
there was one thing better than to
lead a good life, and that was to be
saved from leading any life whatever.

—Thomas Hardy, *Tess of the d'Urbervilles*

All laughing comes from misapprehension.
Rightly looked at, there is no
laughable thing under the sun.

—Thomas Hardy, *Jude the Obscure*

PART ONE
By Tess

PROLOGUE

(The Theory of Adjectives)

I really hate to brag, but I think Jude and I are unhappy. The desire to just get away from everything has got to be the most common symptom of unhappiness. I know it's totally stupid, but unhappy people genuinely believe they can leave their problems behind, they can fix everything with a change of scenery, or by starting over from scratch, or by going off to find themselves, all that crap. ("An' live off the fatta the lan'. An' have rabbits. Go on, George! Tell about what we're gonna have in the garden and about the rabbits in the cages and about the rain in the winter and the stove, and how thick the cream is on the milk like you can hardly cut it. Tell about that, George.")

Okay, so in our case we're not exactly talking about starting over, since all we want to do is go and spend a month in Bird-in-Hand, Pennsylvania, but that should be enough for us because we're only a little bit unhappy. We're only ever a little bit anything. When I told Jude—"Man, I think we're really unhappy!"—he laughed in my face and called me a goth.

"So you reckon we're happy then?"

"God, no! Where the hell did you get that idea?"

And that's how he came to tell me his theory, in considerable detail: according to him, adjectives were created for the sole purpose of describing a tiny handful of people, extreme cases. We use them because they're handy or because we're lazy, but if we ever bothered to stop and think about it, we'd soon realize that the vast majority of people don't really warrant them. We go around saying, "So-and-so is superintelligent," or, more often, "So-and-so is an imbecile," but in reality we hardly ever meet superintelligent people. Or imbeciles, come to that. There are some complete idiots, of course—just as there's the odd genius, a Leonardo da Vinci, at the other end of the spectrum—but these maestros of stupidity are about as rare as babies born with teeth or people born blind. The vast majority of people you come across on a daily basis have never had an original thought in their lives, but they're nonetheless perfectly capable of doing a sudoku in the newspaper. By the same token, people are hardly ever really ugly or really beautiful. They're just nondescript, and the only way to find them interesting is with alcohol or rose-tinted glasses, or some combination of the two. (That's what Jude says. As for me, even when I'm pissed out of my tiny mind, I never get overly excited about anyone.) Jude admits these things aren't always equally distributed. There's always more people at the negative end of the spectrum: more idiots than geniuses, more ugly ducklings than hotties, and, of course, more unhappy people than happy ones. But according to him, it's not unhappiness that's our problem. We've got quite a ways to go if we want to claim to be unhappy. I find this reassuring.

✗ ··· 1 ··· ✗

A LITTLE HISTORY

(Introducing My Topic)

Around the end of the third century, while Emperor Maximian was staying at Octodurum (today Martigny in Switzerland) and finding it somewhat dull, he decided to entertain himself by persecuting some local Christians. His own guards proving insufficient to the task, he called in a Theban legion for reinforcement. The commanding officers of this legion, upon learning the nature of their mission, refused to carry out the emperor's orders and came to a standstill in the narrow passes of Agaunum. Maximian then commanded the decimation of the legion by gladiator sword. When the remaining soldiers still refused to comply, the emperor carried out a second decimation. After the legion sent a delegation to Maximian indicating their resolve not to break the oaths they'd made to God, regardless of how many decimations were commanded, the emperor ordered the legion's massacre.

The brave officers who chose to die with their men rather than attack their fellow Christians were called Maurice, Candidus, and Exuperius. I don't know if the last two were canonized, since I know of no place called Saint Candidus or Saint Exuperius (after all, if your name is Candidus or Exuperius, you can hardly expect anyone to name too many places after you), but what we do know is that Maurice did make it into the liturgical calendar, and has today given his name to a ton of villages, municipalities, regions, and out-of-the-way spots all over the Western world. But whose idea was it to name our own beautiful region in honour of a third-century Theban general? Nobody's. The Saint-Maurice River (and, consequently, the Mauricie region around it) took its name, somewhat ridiculously, from one Maurice Poulin de la Fontaine, who cleared the land in the middle of the seventeenth century. (Which means that my telling you the story of Saint Maurice was pretty much pointless, but I'm confident you'll find some way of dropping it into conversation in the near future.) Monsieur Poulin de la Fontaine was gazing contemplatively at the river one day, after a hard day's work, when he said to himself, "Hang on, this river hasn't been named yet. What if I named it after myself? It's basically my only chance to make sure it isn't forgotten. And just to ensure it doesn't come across as a sin of pride, I'll put a Saint in front of it. There must be a Saint Maurice somewhere. Given that there's a Saint Mechtilde, a Saint Euphrasia, a Saint Euloge, and a Saint Crispin, it would be pretty crazy if after all that time we couldn't dredge up a Maurice or two who'd been chopped into pieces for the glory of Christ." Or perhaps it didn't happen quite like that; maybe Monsieur Poulin de la Fontaine didn't say that to himself at all. In any case, Maurice gave his name to the river, and the river gave it to the region (so that anecdote about Monsieur de Laviolette pulling up to the future site of the town of Trois-Rivières and exclaiming, "By Jove, it's dead here!" must be apocryphal).

It took another two centuries for the region to be settled properly. In 1889, while across the pond Jack the Ripper was rampaging through Whitechapel murdering prostitutes, construction of the Eiffel Tower was almost completed and Germany had just crowned its last emperor, Mr. John Foreman was constructing a hydraulic power station near Shawinigan to power his pulp mill. Lacking capital, he was forced to team up with three

Boston gentlemen: John Edward Aldred, John Joyce, and H. H. Melville (yes, the one of Melville Island fame), the same guys who would in 1897 found the Shawinigan Water & Power Company. Nobody knows exactly which of the three had the idea of calling the village Grand-Mère after the rocky island in the middle of the river, but we do know that we can blame an American if we ended up with the second most ridiculous place name in Quebec (yes, we're looking at you, people of Saint-Louis-du-Ha! Ha!). But these American gentlemen truly had a knack for outlandish names. Which is something we've discovered in our travels to the four corners of America.

x ··· 2 ··· x

TRAVELS ON MOUSEBACK

(The Topic Introduction
Is Dragging Somewhat)

One amusing and instructive way of learning about America is exploring the Family Watchdog website (www. family-watchdog.us), a service that allows American citizens to learn whether anyone in their neighbourhood has been convicted of a sex crime. The home page asks for the name of a town. Let's choose one at random: Anchorage, Alaska. A map pops up with a constellation of little coloured squares corresponding to the houses and workplaces of criminals. These offenders are categorized into four types: "offence against children" (in these cases, the criminal's house is represented by a red square, and his workplace, where applicable, by a burgundy square); "rape" ("offender home" in yellow, "offender work" in white); "sexual battery" (do you know what that means?) ("offender home" in light blue, "offender work" in dark blue); and "other offense" ("offender home" in light green, "offender work" in dark green). In cities with a high population density, the map disappears entirely under little coloured squares, which looks very pretty. Seven hundred and twenty-five people have been convicted of sex crimes in Anchorage, in addition to 509 "non-mappable offenders," whatever that might mean. Let's click on a little red square (home of a child rapist) near International Airport Road.

This brings up the photo and ID sheet of one Douglas Dwayne Martin, currently residing at 4521 Cordova Street, Apartment 4, Anchorage, AK 99503, and working for Alaskan Distributor. Mr. Martin (forty-eight years old, five-foot-ten, 160 pounds, white) was convicted on November 9, 2000, of the following charge: "Attempted Sexual Abuse of Minor 1." If we zoom in a bit, we spot a second little red square right in the same place: another pedophile lives in his building, or in the one right next door. Or maybe they're roommates?

Another go? Let's take Dallas. Maybe I'm prejudiced, but I think there might be some good fishing down there... Aaaand I'm not wrong: it's quite the avalanche of little coloured squares. Especially red ones. It's bizarre, you'd think everyone in Dallas spent their leisure time doing nothing but kiddy-fiddling. (And don't forget that the site shows only the ones who got caught...) There's a big circle all around Harry Moss Park, about fifteen reds and one blue ("sexual battery"). Twenty-two sex offenders within a half-mile radius, Family Watchdog tells us. Maybe not the best place to raise your little family. A random click and here comes the photo of one Richard Allen Haskell (7522 Holly Hill, Apartment 3, Dallas, TX 75321; sixty-seven years old, six-foot-four, 219 lbs), who looks, at first sight, like a completely harmless old guy. Let's see what he's accused of: "Possession of child pornography." No doubt it was all just a misunderstanding; he must have downloaded it by mistake while trying to sign in to his email. Old people are useless with computers.

One last one? (Personally, I could spend hours doing this.) Let's try somewhere quiet this time. Hmm, let's see. Aha! Here we go: Cheyenne, Wyoming. Everyone there is chaste and pure, I'd swear to it. Or maybe not. Holy crap! There are perverts in Cheyenne! You're not safe anywhere. Now, who's hiding behind this little green square at the corner of Missile Drive and Round Top Road? None other than Ron Ernest Schneider, a big red-faced guy with a moustache, which didn't hide the smile on his ID photo. Six foot, 310 pounds, a good specimen of a man. You wouldn't have wanted to be in his victim's place on December 12, 2003, when he committed a "third-degree sexual abuse." Going by the date, it might have happened at a work Christmas party. Can you really hold that against him? I mean, who *hasn't* committed a third-degree sexual abuse after one drink too many?

Jude and me, we weren't just about the sex tourism, we also liked wandering aimlessly around the world—particularly around America, in fact, for reasons that will be explained later—thanks to Google Earth, Google Maps, and Bing Maps. For example, you can tour the Gaspésie in twenty minutes, soaring above Highway 132, clicking on the little icons along the way that indicate images uploaded by volunteer contributors. (Thank you to JMRioux for the beautiful photo of Querry Falls in Caplan, to Simore for the view of the Bonaventure quay, to Paul Langlois for having informed us that Mont-Joli is the world capital of outdoor murals. After that, we head west totally at random. We travel thousands of kilometres with one quick movement (just a few centimetres to the left on the mouse pad), ending up near Minneapolis. Then we zoom in on the posh end of town (it's easy to spot tony areas on the map: they're near green spaces and away from highways), and have a nice little jaunt around Kenwood Parkway, a beautiful wide avenue lined with hundred-year-old trees. The house at number 886 is as big as a school! We swoop in front of the Hubert H. Humphrey Metrodome, home of the Twins, we roam the banks of Lake Nokomis, we amble toward downtown, then we head south again. We jump the four hundred kilometres separating Minnesota's metropolis from Des Moines, Iowa. We'd better see what the buzz is down here. Fly low over Grand View University. Not much going on, it's all very peaceful, but let's just note in passing that the Des Moines fire hydrants are yellow. Another crucial piece of information to take up storage space in our brains. There's not much happening on Euclid Avenue either, even though it seems to be one of the town's main commercial streets. Lots of vehicles (trucks in particular), but no pedestrians: apparently strolling is not the done thing in Des Moines. All right, let's tear ourselves away and head west, toward Nebraska. We fly over Omaha without stopping (something tells us that Omaha and Des Moines are much of a muchness) and are heading along Interstate 80 toward Colorado, when a name catches our attention: Cozad. "What's Cozad?" we ask Wikipedia, which speedily tells us that it's a town in Dawson County with 4,163 inhabitants (according to the 2000 census), whose main—if not only—feature is its position on the hundredth meridian. A huge sign on the way into town points this out. We double-click randomly on Meridian Street, just to check, for surely the people at Google Street View won't have taken their photographerly zeal to such an extent as to photograph the streets of Cozad. But look, believe it or not, that's exactly what they have done. And what does Cozad look like? Meh! Bungalows, commercial buildings, cars, more bungalows, a municipal airport, a few factories, and yet more bungalows. And if you really must know every single detail, the people at 60 Gatewood Drive were about to do some landscaping when the picture was taken. There's a tractor in the alley and a Werner's Sprinklers truck parked in front of the house. And that's the juiciest piece of local gossip we could winkle out. We leave Nebraska and carry on in a southwesterly direction, skipping over Colorado, where no place names catch our eye, and head into Arizona airspace. Right by the New Mexico border there's a godforsaken little place by the name of Fort Defiance (a little over four thousand inhabitants, ninety-two per cent of whom are Navajo Indians). We try to see what it looks like on the ground, but there's nothing to see. Here we have one of those rare places snubbed by Google Street View; when you think that they went to Cozad and Saint-Georges-de-Champlain, it's pretty insulting to the people of Fort Defiance. Now we'll never know what Water Tank Road looks like. Too bad. Anyway, we've had our fill of the back of beyond: let's go and look around downtown Phoenix. Returning to civilization will do us good. But nooo! Phoenix is super-ugly, like Trois-Rivières West with palm trees.

These American small towns are like episodes of *The Young and the Restless*: once you've seen one, you've seen them all. But it never dragged; we'd stay up late in front of the screen, roaming the streets of Edmond and spying on downtown Oklahoma City via the webcam on the roof of city hall, going into raptures every time a passerby appeared in the frame. It wasn't exactly that we despised ordinary cities—Rochester, Cape Breton Regional Municipality, Harrisburg, or any of those charmless, functional agglomerations you only ever hear about on the sports channels ("The Washington Nationals have called up outfielder Manolo Perez from their minor-league team, Harrisburg")—but we did have a particular predilection for places with stupid names. As soon as we saw one that caught our attention (pro tip: fly low if you want to find them; it's usually the small places that have moronic names, and if you fly too high over the map, only the names of big places will show up), we'd stop there and spend some time wandering the main streets. Next we'd go and ask Wikipedia everything there was to know about the place. Most of the time, there wasn't much to say (Chocolate Bayou, Texas, has the nerve to call itself that without any explanation as to why; ditto for Scissors and Ugly), but every once in a while we'd come across a fantastic story.

Here's an example: at the beginning of the fifties, the radio program *Truth or Consequences* was one of the most popular in the United States. One day, the host, Ralph Edwards, announced that the program would be broadcast from the first town that agreed to change its name to Truth or Consequences. The town of Hot Springs, New Mexico (so called because of the many thermal springs in the surrounding area), took up the challenge and is today called Truth or Consequences. As promised, Mr. Edwards and his team moved in and set up shop there. This story, told in a 1997 film, must have inspired the smartasses at Half. com, a virtual garage-sale site. In 2000, they managed to convince the municipal council of Halfway, a small Oregon village of 345 residents, to change its name to Half.com—all in return for a few trinkets (twenty-odd computers for the local primary school, a free website, etc.). "We were talking about how to get the company on the map, and we said: "Why don't we get on the map. Literally," declared the site's founder, Josh Kopelman, proud of the stunt.

When the town of Climax, Minnesota, was established in 1896, it was, without any ulterior motive, given the name of its main employer, a chewing-tobacco manufacturer. Nobody could have predicted that the word *climax* would one day become synonymous with *orgasm* in everyday language. Once the harm had been done, the only option for the town's 243 inhabitants was to pretend nothing was up, which didn't always work out too well. Take, for example, that day in 2004 when the high school principal sent a student home for contravening, according to her, the school's dress code by wearing a T-shirt printed with a message with sexual connotations. She didn't know that the phrase in question was, quite simply, the town's new slogan ("Climax, more than just a feeling!"), which had come out on top in a local contest. Among the finalists, other suggestions included "No end to Climax" and "Bring a friend to Climax."

In Arizona there's a place called Why. Why? Well, to start off with, the town was known by the name Y because routes 85 and 86 joined up there, making a Y shape. However, because Arizona law stipulates that town names must have a minimum of three letters, the town councillors were requested to comply without delay. After some discussion, they opted for Why, which of course sounds the same as the letter Y. Let's just point out for the record that the route of these two roads has been changed, and the junction today looks like a T.

At the beginning of the nineteenth century, most of what is today the state of Michigan was inhabited by Indians from the Potawatomi tribe. Toward the end of the 1830s, the first white settlers arrived, and by 1840 they were sufficiently numerous to justify constructing a school, the area around which quickly became built up. One George Reeves, owner of both the general store and a distillery, was considered the founder of this town, so it was to him that the authorities went to ask for an official place name. "You can name it Hell, for all I care," came the response. On October 13, 1841, the town was officially named Hell.

Chicken, Alaska, started out as a mining camp that, for its first century of existence, had no official name and was none the worse for it. When they built a post office there in 1902, the US Postal Service informed the population (thirty-seven people spread over six households, according to the last census), that their tiny backwater would have to be christened in order for mail to be delivered there. As there were a lot of ptarmigans in the area, they decided to call the place Ptarmigan. However, at the time of completing the incorporation request, nobody could agree on the spelling of the word. In desperation, the mayor (or whoever it was) asked if anyone could suggest a different bird name. "Chicken!" was the first suggestion heard, and as everyone was in a rush to get the chore over with and go home, Chicken it was.

In the "It would have been better not to know" category, who could not feel slightly disappointed upon learning that the town of Boring, Oregon, is so named simply because it was founded by one W. H. Boring? That You Bet, California, was christened in honour of the favourite expression of the guy who owned the saloon back then? That Uncertain, Texas, takes its name from the fact that when Texas was an independent state, the residents were for a period of time uncertain of their citizenship, the border between the United States and the Republic of Texas being much disputed? Or that Ninety Six, South Carolina, was so named for the simple reason that it was situated ninety-six miles from the important city of Keowee?

This next one is the best: in 1869 the inhabitants of a small Texas colony decided to incorporate and demanded a post office from the US Postal Service. Unfortunately, the name they'd chosen for their town was rejected. (We don't know what this name was, nor the reasons for its rejection.) The councillors of the future Nameless, somewhat irritated, nevertheless yielded to the decision and submitted another name, which was also rejected. This was a little harder to swallow, but they didn't let it get them down. They brainstormed once more and submitted a third name, which, just like the first two, failed to please the post-office bureaucrats. This circus was repeated no less than six times. After the sixth rejection, the good colonists jokingly returned the form with the following inscription: "Let the post office be nameless and damned!" They were taken at their word, and in 1880 the town was registered with the name of Nameless. What I want to know is, what were the six rejected names? What could merit a no when they said yes to Coupon, Elephant, Unicorn, Comfort, Finger, Frog Jump, Defeated, Double Trouble, Good Intent, Loveladies, Perfection, Purchase, Burnt Chimney Corner, Duck, Elf, Hairtown, Lower Pig Pen, Upper Pig Pen, Meat Camp, Othello, Poor Town, Pope Crossing, Spies, Brilliant, Coolville, Dull, Liars Corner, Loveland, Pee Pee, America, Box, Cement, Chance, Frogville, Okay, Pink, Poop Creek, Remote, Sweet Home, Dynamite, Index, Triangle, Zaza, Domestic, New Discovery, Zulu, Ginseng, Hell for Certain, Hippo, King Arthur's Court, Satan's Kingdom, Krypton, Lovely, Miracle, Normal, and Ordinary?

x ··· 3 ··· x

THE MOST BEAUTIFUL GIRL
IN ROUYN-NORANDA

Being armchair tourists suited us down to the ground. We used to say that it would be cool to actually go somewhere, to feel the Pimlico breeze on our skin, to go shopping in downtown Happyland, to make friends in Dirty Butter Creek, but we both knew it was all just hot air, and we were always careful to add "whenever we can make it work" or "when we've got the cash." Another way of saying never. And if we ever happened to come up with a question that was outside Google's rather vast field of competence, such as "I wonder what the most beautiful girl in Rouyn-Noranda is called," we pondered it for a few moments before dismissing the idea, saying, "Oh well, too bad we'll never know." One day (I think we were farting around in Brazil, Indiana), I can't really remember what we were talking about, but I said, "We should totally go there," and I was astonished by the conviction in my own voice. Jude could have neutralized it by kidding around, like he does every time it looks like I might be getting serious, but instead he replied in the same tone. Yeah, we should totally go there. Our eyes met for a fraction of a second, then we moved on to talk about something else, but nonetheless we knew we'd just taken a serious decision.

Here, the reader might be tempted to say, "Hold your horses, Ben-Hur! Don't you think it's overstating the case to call a vague travel plan a serious decision?" To which I reply that if you knew us a bit better, dear reader, you'd know that from our point of view a decision is by definition serious, that decisions are something we avoid like the plague. By the time I've decided which pair of socks to put on and what to spread on my toast, I've pretty much reached my quota of decisions for the day. You should also know that we're the kind of people to make a mountain out of a molehill. We don't try to hide it. Most of the time, we don't even need the molehill. We've never accomplished anything, never been anywhere, and the smallest change in our routine pushes us to the brink of despair. What you, dear reader, might call an "annoying setback," a "little glitch," a "minor irritation," or "last-minute change," we would call the apocalypse. We're not going to change; it's too late, given our ages, and it'll probably get worse. But all the same we'll go to Bird-in-Hand; of that I can assure you. (Bird-in-Hand is in Pennsylvania, but let's not put the cart before the horse.)

From the moment we knew we'd be going on a trip, we started confining ourselves to the Americas. Now that the whole point of our virtual wanderings was to find our ideal destination, now that we were no longer content just to rove randomly around, we no longer saw the point of getting all the info about Rue du Grand-Puits in Saint-Yrieix-sur-Charent (in the Angoulême suburbs), or about Shanghai's Zhujiang Gardens. We had to be realistic: we knew full well we'd never dare put an ocean between ourselves and home. If you found yourself in a bind in Lowell, for example, you could always hitchhike, steal a bike, or at worst walk. Terry Fox crossed Canada on foot—we're no crazier than him. On the other hand, if the sticky situation cropped up in Chepek (Turkmenistan) or some part of Aden (Yemen), what would you do? You'd curl up in a ball in the corner and cry while you waited to die. The United States offers the best change-of-scene-to-safety ratio. And on that note, I'm going to start a new chapter to explain just how we came to choose Bird-in-Hand.

x ··· 4 ··· x

AUTHOR INTRODUCTION
(Because It's Important
to Do Things Properly)

As the chapter title indicates, I've changed my mind: I'm not going to tell you about Bird-in-Hand right away. Just above, I said, "If you knew us a bit better, dear reader, blah blah blah…," which made me realize we've gotten twenty or so pages in and I have yet to say anything about myself. I have no desire to be well-known, but it seems to me that the reader, who has (or so I hope) paid good money for this book, has the right to know who they're dealing with.

Mr. Marc Fisher, in his indispensable work *Advice to a Young Writer*, recommends introducing the characters bit by bit as the narrative progresses. ("Aerate the information," as he so nicely puts it.) Reveal their motivation and personality through dialogue or, better still, by making them act. Possessing neither the craft nor the master's fiendish talent, I'll make do with presenting everything in one go. After that, we'll be done with this chore and we can get into the meat of the subject. All right, let's get on with it. My name's Tess, I'm thirty-two, and I live in Grand-Mère with Jude, whom I will let introduce himself when it's his turn to write. Now I have to tell you what I do for a living. I work at Subway (just across from Petro-Canada, you know the one). I make subs according to customers' wishes, I ask them if it's for here or to go, whether it's just the sub or a combo. If the latter, I ask them if they want a cookie or chips. After that, I take their payment. When there aren't any customers, I fill the little ingredient containers, I cut tomatoes or cucumbers, I wipe down tables with a rag, that sort of thing. It's not overly taxing, but it's not something you'd do for fun. Now what? What do you talk about when you've told someone your name, age, place of residence, and profession? (Take the lack of quotation marks around that last word as a bit of black humour.) I don't know. Any questions? Hmmm... Let's see, why don't we try this another way. Give me a couple of minutes and I should be able to track down an online personality test, which I will fill in before your very eyes.

Aha! This one seems good: "Help Your Friends Get to Know You Better in Fifty Questions." For the sake of the test, we'll pretend you're my friend, which will be weird. Most of the questions are a bit dumb, so I'll spare you them. But the answers should help you figure out who I am.

Help Your Friends Get to Know You Better
(questionnaire found at www.sedecouvrir.fr, completed by Tess for the reader's edification)

1. 22:06
2. Tess
3. 32
4. I don't know exactly.
    Somewhere around five foot four.
5. Brown
6. Brown
7. Aquarius
8. Grand-Mère
9. One sister

10. No

11. Yes, Sébastien Daoust (according to him)

12. Nothing at all

13. Texas Chain Saw Massacre

14. In Search of Lost Time

15. "I Think We're Alone Now"

16. A Haunting

17. Quiet

18. Disagreeable

19. No

20. A naked girl

21. Country

22. Winter

23. Exactly where I am now

24. Go to Bird-in-Hand

25. Jude

26. No

27. I'd choose the dead one

28. A photo of Virginia Woolf

29. The floor

30. Sushi

31. I don't think I have one

32. No

33. In Bird-in-Hand

34. I don't give a shit

35. Nobody

36. "You know what?"

37. The doorbell ringing

38. To the neighbour just now,
    but that doesn't really count

39. No

40. No

41. Rasputin

42. Barbed wire around my arm or a tramp
    stamp on the small of my back, just like
    everyone else
43. None
44. I've never voted
45. Nothing really
46. Boil water for coffee
47. Take out my contacts
48. Never, that only happens to other people
49. Not excessively
50. 22:31

There, now we're bosom buddies. Let's get on with the serious stuff.

x ··· 5 ··· x

BIRD-IN-HAND

If you believe the people at Google Maps (and personally I find them infallible), it takes exactly nine hours and forty-seven minutes to get to Bird-in-Hand by car. Of course, they aren't taking into account pee breaks, nor the fact that you might want to stop for a snack in Albany, but since they imagine that you'll stick rigidly to the speed limit, the latter compensates for the former.

Leaving our house (just next to Laflèche College, to give you an idea), you take Sixth to the end and then continue on Beech Street, which turns into Boulevard Saint-Sacrement and then, later on, Champlain Avenue. Why didn't they just call it Beech Street all the way along? Good question. Maybe because there aren't any beeches along part of the route, or perhaps they were loath to give Champlain an entire street, given that he never set foot in Shawinigan. Go figure. Anyway, you turn right at the top of Trudel and follow Highway 55 to the Trois-Rivières exit. You take said highway (but don't forget to give it back! Lol!) and get off it after nearly thirty kilometres to take Highway 40 toward Montreal. In the outskirts of the metropolis, follow the signs for the Louis-Hippolyte-LaFontaine Bridge–Tunnel. Before going in, you'll see a traffic sign forbidding big black squares: make sure you haven't got a big black square on your car. (Anyone get the joke?) Once out of the tunnel, take Highway 20 south, which soon becomes the 132, before changing once more and becoming Highway 15, if I've understood correctly. The Google directions are a bit confusing for this part of the route, but it's clearer when you see it on the map. Basically, drive south and, before you know it, you'll hit the American border. There, the customs officer will ask suspiciously why you've come to the States.

"We're going to Bird-in-Hand, sir!"

"Oh! Welcome then."

This formality dealt with, you carry on south on Highway 15, which by the way is no longer called that but now has the catchier name of Adirondack Northway/Interstate 87 S. Enjoy the countryside for 280 kilometres, then take 1 W toward New York/Buffalo. It's around here that the Albany snack stop I mentioned comes in. If you aren't hungry I won't force you, but just so you know, you've been driving for almost five hours; it would do you good to stretch your legs. Do you like oysters? If so, get yourself to Jack's Oyster House (42–44 State Street, Albany, NY 12207), which seems to have an excellent reputation in the area. Sure, it's a bit fancy, but for your first meal abroad surely you can indulge in a little treat. Besides, they sell other things besides oysters. The establishment is run by a "French Certified MasterChef" by the name of Luc Pasquier, who makes just about everything: Massachusetts cod in granola crumble on a bed of Meyer lemon emulsion, or classic chicken schnitzel, or duck à l'orange braised with candied zest, etc.

Right, now you're full. Let's jump back in the car. Interstate 287 S will take you into New Jersey, but you'll skip straight through it (and with good reason: New Jersey is basically the American Mississauga). After just three-quarters of an hour, take exit 21B onto Interstate 78, and there you are in Pennsylvania, the cradle of American democracy. You'll feel beat (especially if you opted for a glass or two of Riesling to wash the oysters down), but you need to stay alert because it gets a bit confusing at this point, Bird-in-Hand being located some distance from the main highways. Short version: you'll go down a few secondary roads and after an hour of tootling around you'll get to the outskirts of Lancaster, the biggest town between Philadelphia and Pittsburgh (Lancaster's 500,000 inhabitants make it the hundred-and-first-biggest city in the country, no less…). After Lancaster, drive east on Old Philadelphia Pike (also called, more prosaically, Road 340) for just half an hour and, voilà, there you are! Welcome to Bird-in-Hand! When you see the sign with its bird in a hand, you exclaim to your passenger, "Here we are at last!"

"Finally! I don't care what anyone says, nine hours and forty-seven minutes in the car is hell on your butt."

"Thank goodness we stopped at Albany for that snack."

"Totally!"

If you don't have a passenger, you can say all that in your head. Next, you start looking for somewhere to stay. The first place you spot, on your right, the Bird-in-Hand Family Inn, would do perfectly well, but you could also head down to the Amish Country Motel, the Mill Stream Country Inn, or even the Travelers Rest Motel. The best thing about all this is that you won't upset anybody by choosing one over the other since they all belong to the Smucker family, the local big shots. Be that as it may, I nonetheless recommend the Bird-in-Hand Family Inn, because it's located right next to the Bird-in-Hand Family Restaurant & Smorgasbord, also owned by the Smuckers, where they serve traditional Lancaster County meals. Which means what? I must confess I don't entirely know what they mean by that. On the photo decorating the menu (on the town's website: www.bird-in-hand.com), you can see a big ham, a stuffed turkey, peas, mashed potatoes, pies, pastries, and a basket of fried things, all under the rapturous eyes of a little redheaded girl (a little Smucker?) biting into a corncob. It looks delicious, but I wouldn't like to see the arteries of someone who ate that every day. However, once is not a habit, and Albany's oysters were a long way back, so go ahead, stuff your face at the smorgasbord (which appears to be the Amish way of saying all-you-can-eat). Next: a shower and a good night's sleep before setting off to explore Bird-in-Hand.

Bird-in-Hand was officially founded in 1836, but there was a coaching inn there as far back as the beginning of the eighteenth century. This establishment, which belonged to a couple comprising Mr. William McNabb and his wife, Dorothy, was called, quite simply, Hotel McNabb, as proven by the pretty sign decorating the front window. Under the business name in gothic font, the artist has drawn, according to either the McNabbs' instructions or his own imagination, a hand holding a little red bird. Why a bird in a hand? History doesn't tell us, but if, like me, you are blessed with a lot of free time and a penchant for useless information, it won't take you long to discover that there's an English expression, originating in a song from 1781 ("Sung at Vauxhall"), that goes, "One bird in the hand is worth two in the bush." Which is approximately equivalent to the French "Un tiens vaut mieux que deux que tu l'auras," or even of that wise verse in Ecclesiastes, which has it that a live dog is worth more than a dead lion. But as "Sung at Vauxhall" dates from 1781 and Mr. McNabb was running his business around 1715, that doesn't get us very far, except for demonstrating my great erudition or my skill at typing words into a search engine. However, to complicate matters further, we note that this idea of a bird in the hand being worth more than two in the bush goes much further back. It was around 1530, in his book *The Boke of Nurture, or School of Good Manners*, that Hugh Rhodes wrote, "A byrd in hand—is worth ten flye at large." But in this case it might rather mean you shouldn't have more than one iron in the fire, since "byrd" here means a member of the female sex.

In short, for one reason or another, there was a bird in a hand on William McNabb's hotel sign. And since at that time the place was frequented by settlers from all the countries of Europe (especially Germans and Dutch) who barely spoke English (and read it even less), and since even those whose mother tongue was English were by and large illiterate, what they took from the sign was the drawing. Thus came the custom of designating the place as Bird-in-Hand (or Oiseau dans la main, or Vogel in der Hand, or Pájaro en mano, or птица в рука, etc.). In any case, at the time, all the coaching inns along the Old Philadelphia Pike were named after the pictures on their signs or, failing that, after some geographical particularity or other. You find places like The Ship, The Wagon, The Plough, The Buck, White Horse, Black Horse, The Hat, etc. It seems, though, that Bird-in-Hand is the only one of these place names to have come down through time to appear on the maps of today.

However, when the post-office mafia got involved and demanded that the town be given an official name, it was given the name Enterprise (yes, like the starship). Why? I can't find the answer to that anywhere, but I guess it was because of some grumpy official (possibly the same one who inflicted misery on the people of Nameless) who thought that Bird-in-Hand wasn't serious enough. But Enterprise or no, everyone brazenly carried on calling the place Bird-in-Hand, to the extent that in 1873 the authorities agreed to go along with this done deal, and the town was entered into the state records under its real name.

For a long time, Bird-in-Hand was basically little more than a market. The nearby Amish came there to sell their products a couple of times a week, then went back to their farms. On non-market days, it was essentially a ghost town, with a population that barely made it to three figures. Things changed in 1911, when Jonathan Stoltzfus bought a sixty-acre farm in the area. Later on, his sons opened a hotel and started developing tourism in the region. Today, his descendants (the Smuckers) own just about all the town's businesses. You're going to say, "If the guy was called Stoltzfus, why would his descendants be called Smucker?" Well, Smucker sounds more American, which is better for business. Simple as that.

x ··· **6** ··· x

WHY BIRD-IN-HAND?

That, dear reader, is an excellent question. You've no doubt noticed that I used it for the title of this chapter. It gives me less to come up with, and gives you the impression of being a part of things. So, why Bird-in-Hand…?

I'd be lying if I said it was based on a rational decision. In fact, the first answer that comes to mind is "just because." But since that isn't acceptable in a text with literary ambitions, I'll attempt to come up with an explanation. I'll begin by pointing out that a fair bit of time passed between that notable evening when we decided to go somewhere and the moment of our first move. Not our strong point, making a move. My sister says that if the word *vacillatory* didn't exist, she'd have had to invent it just for us. But she's wrong, and anyway she just says that to show off one of the only big words she knows. *Vacillatory* means that you fully intend to do something, but you can never make up your mind to get on with it; well, I can swear to you that we've never been the least vacillatory. And if you think our trip to Pennsylvania falls into that category, it'll be time to eat your words when our postcard arrives.

Our first move, then, was to choose a destination (and yes, that does count as a move). To start with, we were only thinking about Connecticut. First of all, the distance seemed just right. It's about seven hundred kilometres from here to Hartford (a few more or less, depending on which route you choose, but seven hundred exactly going by Interstate 87), which is far enough to feel as though you've gone away, yet close enough to not induce a panic attack. We'd established that our mental limit was a thousand kilometres. (Bird-in-Hand, at 980 kilometres from Grand-Mère, just sneaks in.) But the main thing about Connecticut is that that's where the fictional Stars Hollow is, where Rory and Lorelai Gilmore live. Sure, it's a made-up town, and probably *The Gilmore Girls* wasn't really even filmed in Connecticut, but we still love that state. So Connecticut then, but where exactly? Mystic? Crystal Lake? Wolcott? Moosup? Canaan? All those towns tempted us at one time or another but, as they say on *Highlander,* "There can be only one." At one point, without really thinking about it, I burst out with, "Oh, fuck it, let's just go to Bird-in-Hand and be done with it." Jude replied, "Well, yes, of course that's what we should do, for fuck's sake," and we burst out laughing. Deal done. We joke around, but joking is our way of being serious.

We knew the name from having seen it between Bald Head and Camel Hump on those lists of "funny place names," "strange city names," and other "weird town names" we couldn't get enough of. It was just another stupid place name, uncommon enough to merit inclusion in these lists, but not weird enough for us to be really intrigued. However, we took it as a sign that it popped into my mind out of the blue. Right away we roped in our favourite search engines (by the by, according to Family Watchdog, no sexual predators are listed in the town) and, after a few short hours, we knew as much about Bird-in-Hand as if we'd been born there.

x ··· 7 ··· x

A PROBLEM WELL-STATED

Whichever way you look at it, there are basically two things we need to get this project up and running: a car and some money. And since cars cost money, we can simplify things further and say that all we're short of is some dough. We've worked out that we need between $10,000 and $15,000 (including the cost of the car) to finance the trip. They say that a problem well-stated is a problem halfway solved, but something tells me it might not be the easiest half.

My important job in the submarine industry brings in roughly a thousand dollars a month. (Twenty-five hours per week at nearly ten dollars an hour: do the math.) You'll say, "You just need to work more, you lazybones, then your pockets would be a bit fuller." At first glance that seems like good advice, but it doesn't actually work like that: if I worked more, I'd become a taxpayer, and I'd end up worse off overall. To really earn more money, I'd have to work a *lot* more, something like forty hours a week. And I know myself well enough to know that twenty-five hours is the upper limit of what I can stand. The Grand-Mère Subway might not be the busiest in the world, and I might earn my salary simply by standing behind the counter and rearranging the chips rack to save face with the manager, but I frequently come within a hair's breadth of walking out right in the middle of making a sub. Sometimes I dream about it so much that I think I'm really doing it. Yes, I know I'm a wimp, and I know everyone's talking about Chinese people in China who slave eighteen hours a day for fifty cents an hour so we can buy nice trinkets at Dollarama, but that's completely irrelevant. The main thing to remember is that my job brings in a thousand dollars a month.

You and the rest of the taxpayers, in your infinite generosity, subsidize Jude to the tune of just under six hundred dollars a month, via the Ministry of Social Services, for which he is exceedingly appreciative. Our total income therefore comes to $1,600 a month. As far as fixed expenses go, our rent is $425 and the folks at Hydro-Québec send us a bill for seventy-five dollars every month, which brings us to a nice round five hundred for a roof over our heads and the certainty that something will happen when we flick a switch. We spend around $200 on groceries, not including beer. (Add another hundred.) That's basically it for our fixed costs. (We hook up to the internet by stealing Wi-Fi from someone called Doum37, and as for cable, this guy Mario (the neighbour's friend) installed it illegally for sixty bucks.

In short, half of our income is dedicated to our basic needs. And the rest of it? It goes up in smoke, evaporates, vanishes into thin air. Pitchers at Chez Véro, crappy celebrity mags, trinkets. Of course, we could save money by choosing to drink at home and by not knowing in intimate detail the love life of the *Twilight* cast, but, even then, we'd only save a few hundred dollars each month. At that rate, it would take three or four years to reach our goal. And we don't want to set off in three or four years, we want to go really soon.

A double room at the Bird-in-Hand Family Inn costs exactly $127.65 per night. With meals and minor expenses, we reckon we'd be spending around $250 a day, so about fifteen hundred a week. With $10,000, we could hold out for a month and a half, but we'd need to keep some kind of safety net for coming home, because there's no guarantee my boss would still like me if I decided to take six weeks of unpaid leave; he could easily decide to replace me by whoever's CV was at the top of the pile. (Note that this isn't a prospect I find overly dismaying.) We could also expect to spend a thousand dollars all told on gas, and four thousand for the car. That seems to be the minimum you need to spend on a vehicle to be sure of avoiding problems. You can always try to be crafty and buy an old beater for $300, but you're no further ahead if it all falls to pieces two days later. That's not my opinion, I'm quoting (pretty much verbatim) Jude's dad, who knows his way around cars. He also told us, "If you want to go to the States, it's good to have a sensible car, because sometimes they won't even let you over the border if you're driving a clunker. I don't know if that's true, but better not to risk it. Plus, we don't love the idea of breaking down at the side of Interstate 87 and spending the day sitting next to a gumball machine in some garage in Keeseville, Vermont, while the mechanic talks to us in English, licking his lips every time he looks at us because it's written all over our faces that we know diddly-squat about cars. So we'll buy ourselves a decent car, even if we end up selling it when we get back, if we haven't got too attached to it.

x ··· 8 ··· x

SOME BAD IDEAS

It was only at the end of a long brainstorming session, during which all the schemes for getting rich quick were investigated and rejected one by one, that we developed a more or less workable plan. At school, whenever we organized a brainstorming session (or a "brain stirring," as we called it then), the teacher used to say, "When you're brain-stirring, there are no bad ideas. You need to get everything down and then sort it out later." She'd have eaten her words if she'd been there with us. It was a total bad-ideas fest. Here's an excerpt, to give you some idea.

Jude: I've got it! A pyramid scheme.

Me: Nobody makes money on pyramid schemes, except the guy at the top of the pyramid.

Jude: Obviously it would be our pyramid, so we'd be at the top, so it would be our pockets getting full.

Me: Except that to start a pyramid, you need to convince five of your friends to sign up, who then have to convince five of their friends, etc. Think about it: have we even got five friends?

Jude: Yeah, that's a problem. The lottery then?

Me: Are you serious?

Jude: Yes, hear me out. The chance of hitting on the winning number in the 6/49 are one in 12 million. One ticket costs two dollars. You with me?

Me: So far, so good.

Jude: Right, so that means that to play all 12 million possible combinations, you'd need to spend 24 million. You just wait until the top prize is higher than that, and play every combination. Even if it's only 25 million, you've still got a million dollars profit.

Me: That's so easy! And we wonder why there are still any poor people in Quebec. And if someone else has chosen the winning numbers and you have to share your 25 million, you're down 12 million.

Jude: Eleven point five.

Me: Fine. But just out of curiosity, where do you get the 24 million to start with?

Jude: All right, I give up. Your turn to suggest something.

Me: Um… we could sell an organ we don't need on the black market. A kidney, say. We have two, but you can manage perfectly well with just the one.

Jude: Where would you find an organ trafficker?

Me: Same place you find everything—the internet.

Jude: You're full of shit. You're telling me you'd seriously be game to go to some illegal operating theatre in some basement apartment to be put to sleep by a Chinese man who sterilizes his instruments with Jack Daniel's?

Me: You racist! Why would he be Chinese?

Jude: Dunno. Some film I've seen, I guess… Anyway, answer me: you'd be up for it?

Me: No.

Jude: We could open a massage parlour with extras.

Me: What kind?

Jude: The kind where the customer pays eighty dollars for an hour's Thai massage and twenty dollars more if he wants an extra.

Me: And I'm guessing it would be me dispensing these

massages...

Jude: Yes. Well, you are a girl.

Me: Indeed I am. Absolutely no way, but I do have a couple questions. No, make that three. One: how come you know the going rate in this kind of establishment? Two: what is a "Thai" massage? Three: what's the "extra"?

Jude: As to your first question, the internet again. What did you think? A Thai massage is when the girl rubs her breasts on the customer, and the extra is a hand job.

Me: I don't have breasts, so that settles that problem.

Jude: Do you think the Petro-Canada cashier would recognize us if we wore masks?

Etc.

It went on like that for a good two hours. Discouraged by how pathetic we were, we were going to throw in the towel, adjourn the meeting until the following day, when we stumbled across the Idea of the Century. (That's what we called our just about workable plan, to give us hope.) It pains me to write it, and nobody would ever know if I tampered with the truth a little; nevertheless, my conscience obliges me to confess that the Idea of the Century came from the neighbour. (No need to introduce the neighbour, he's nobody, some random guy; the only interesting thing about him is the way we got to know him, a pretty incredible story that I won't tell you right away so as not to get too scattered, but I'll find some way of shoehorning it in later on.) So, it was the neighbour who came up with the Idea of the Century. Well, it might be fairer to say that he put us on the right track. There he was, sprawled on the couch while we were stirring our brains, and as usual we weren't paying much attention to his presence or to what he was saying. It actually took us several minutes to realize that he had, contrary to all expectations, suggested something not entirely idiotic, and for us to say, "Come again?" But before I tell you about our idea, I really need to introduce you to Sébastien Daoust, who will play a key role in its implementation.

x···9···x

THE LOCAL LITERARY SCENE

You can accuse me of taking the long way round, of going from Shawinigan to Trois-Rivières via Winnipeg, but I think I'm totally entitled to take this tale wherever I want. It's the author's whim and not up for discussion. If you want to read stories that go from A to B as quickly as possible, breathless tales with a ton of narrative unity (if the term *narrative unity* is too difficult for your little head, you simply have to consult the first work of literary theory, Bakhtin's *Esthétique et théorie du roman*, Henry James's *The Art of the Novel*, or even Marc Fisher's *Advice to a Young Novelist*, from which I've already slipped in a word or two and which will be further dealt with later), if you want a book where something happens, go and buy a John Grisham or a Mary Higgins Clark and leave me in peace. That said, it's true I could sketch a portrait of Sébastien Daoust in a few pencil strokes (all the easier since he's not especially interesting) and then come back to the topic at hand, but the truth is I'm quite happy to have a chance to tell you about the Grand-Mère literary scene, of which Mr. Daoust is only the most modest representative. No kidding, for a town that isn't exactly a megalopolis (around twelve thousand, max), Grand-Mère counts among its inhabitants an impressive number of well-known writers.

Credit where credit's due, let's start our overview with a famous name: Paule Doyon, whose works will, I hope, be familiar to you. If not, abandon your current reading and rush to your bookstore to acquire Ms. Doyon's complete works. If your bookstore claims not to have it in stock, change bookstores. After all, life hangs by a mere thread: you could easily get knocked over by a truck as you come out your front door, you could be struck by lightning, suffer an aneurysm, and you'd be dead without having read Paule Doyon, which is really not the done thing in the afterlife, or so I understand. So, which one should you start with? (We have before us a particularly abundant oeuvre.) I suggest you begin with her sapiential writings, such as her famous *Livre M* (Éditions En Marge), in which she responds definitively to those questions with which the greatest minds have wrestled for two and a half millennia. (What is the meaning of life on earth? Where do we come from? Where are we going?) And all this in a little book of 122 pages, in which she also deals with telepathy, automatic writing, and the possibility of communicating with other planets. Now you know the universe's biggest secrets, you can die in peace. But I implore you to do no such thing and instead make the trek to the author's novelistic universe with *We Need to Talk about Albert* (Stanké), which was a finalist for the Gérald Godin Prize in 1997, and about which Réginald Martel (who is never wrong) said, "This novel has a lot of character, a little humour, and the definitive proof that Ms. Doyon knows how to make her stories exciting right to the very end."

Now, since I like you a lot, I'll tell you a secret (but don't go spreading it around): a significant portion of Paule Doyon's work is available without you even having to get off your ass or lay out any cash: by going to her site (www.cafe.rapidus.net/anddoyon/index.html), you can read poems, tales, short comic pieces, and even a whole novel! You don't believe me? Go and see! Look, just as a teaser, here's a snippet I chose randomly. A little piece in verse written on the occasion of the loss of a loved one. Hold back your tears if you can.

```
No more little dishes
On the parquet floor
Nor black hairballs dozing on the carpet
All the armchairs are empty
And the doors stay closed
The house misses you everywhere . . .

Noir-Noir the cat has softly gone
Far from pain...
In the invisible universe he now sleeps
His velvet paw still trying now and then
To pat my knee . . .
```

I'll give you a few moments to pull yourself together and then I'll go on with another literary heavyweight, Mr. Bryan Perro. (Speaking of heavyweights, and you're going to accuse me again of losing my grip on the subject, especially as we're already in the middle of a digression, but I have to go with it when I think of it, otherwise I lose my ideas. So, speaking of heavyweights, have you noticed that you often hear that writing is a starving-in-a-garret sort of job, but most of the writers you see on television are pretty chubby? Bryan Perro [since we're talking about him]: heavier than all of Alexandre Dumas's characters put together. Victor-Lévy Beaulieu: all the usual words people use to describe his work ["Immense!" "Vast!"] apply equally well to his trousers; Christian Mistral: luckily, coke acts as an appetite suppressant, since without that he'd be big enough to qualify for his own postal code; Michel Brûlé [yes, I am including him as a writer; it's important to be kind]: should be on the blacklist of every buffet owner in the metropolis. There are of course some exceptions, but by and large I'm right.) Anyway, let's get back to the topic at hand: Bryan Perro. The towns of Shawinigan and Saint-Mathieu-du-Parc could argue it with us, since he was born in the first and lives today in the second, but he's important enough in our great town's cultural life to be considered an honorary Grand-Mérois. Since I am not among his target audience, I haven't got much to say about this author (but for anyone interested: www.bryanperro.com), except that he's a perfect example of the saying that the apple never falls far from the tree, Bryan Perro being the son of a certain André Perreault, who wrote for the Saint-Maurice newspaper and amazed us every week by his astonishing ability to cram four hundred adverbs into a five-hundred-word piece.

The Descôteaux family is another Grand-Mère literary dynasty. You'll all remember that famous TV show about the Mauricie region, *Entre chiens et loups*, written by Ms. Aurore Descôteaux between 1985 and 1993, which delighted everyone who found the historical soap *Le temps d'une paix* too intellectual. You will also remember that in this production, the role of Arthur Grandmaison was played with great panache by Gilles Descôteaux, son of the author, whose serious voice and handlebar moustache made him a retirement-home pin-up. What few people know, however, is that when the acting profession dropped Mr. Descôteaux, he reinvented himself as a singer. What does that have to do with literature? I hear you ask. You'll understand the stupidity of that question when you've taken the trouble to read the lyrics of his songs (www.frmusique.ru/texts/d/descoteaux_gilles/descoteaux.htm). We might have to wait until after he's dead, as is so often the case, for this poet of the everyday to get the recognition he deserves, but for now, the fact that he's sold as few CDs as Stendhal sold books during his lifetime only makes him seem better in the eyes of those elite few who understand him. And since I am of course including you in that category, I can't stop myself from ending with a few choice extracts for you. Such as this quatrain, taken from the incredible "To Love You Better":

```
I see you everywhere now in a child's grin
In the lonely tears of a cripple's heart
I see you in the sky I even hear you in the wind
In the greeting of a friend in the song of a
bird
```

And these two, from his masterpiece, "Your Child Is Not Ours":

```
I pick up the things he leaves lying around
I make his bed and fold his clothes
I cater to all of his dietary whims
As a thank-you he laughs in my face

Your child is not ours
But I've accepted him out of love
I wouldn't want to live with another
So my dear let me bring him up.
```

✗···10···✗

SÉBASTIEN DAOUST

So that's pretty much it for the Grand-Mère literary scene. Impressive, right? (I hope in future you'll keep your lips zipped instead of calling us all rednecks.) It's not even an exhaustive list, but the ones I haven't named are just too obscure for me to bother with here. The most obscure of all is undoubtedly Sébastien Daoust, and the only reason I'm including him now is because, as I mentioned before, he plays a part in this story.

The back-cover bio on *The Death of the Pterodactyl* is about as laconic as you can get: "Sébastien Daoust was born in 1972. He studied literature and linguistics at the University of Montreal. He lives in Grand-Mère. *The Death of the Pterodactyl* is his second published work." Having the honour of knowing him personally, I am in a position to be able to fill out this summary with the following information: he lives on Seventh, he works for Doral Marine, and he's in the habit of stopping off at Subway almost every day on his way back from work and slowly savouring a combo while reading the *Journal de Montréal*. And if you really want to know everything, I might add that he has a marked preference for the foot-long meatball sub with a Diet Coke and a macadamia-nut cookie. You're starting to figure me out, so you know I'm not really the type to flirt with customers, and if it was left to me, I'd never have discovered that this big, placid boy, with his glasses and his receding hairline, had earned a PhD in literature when he defended, in 2002, a thesis entitled *Time in Paul Valéry: A Poetics of Perception* (talk about a man dealing with real problems!) and that he had since published two critically acclaimed books.

If I do know all this, it's because Mr. Daoust has a bit of a thing for me. I'm really not saying this to puff myself up, but I have the kind of look that intellectuals and artists like. I look kind of angular and dumb, a combination that seems, for one reason or another, to appeal to intelligent, anguished, annoying guys. I'm never going to be asked to model for a truckers' calendar, but I could be quite the heartbreaker at a poetry soirée. I hadn't been working at Subway for two weeks before I had signed copies of *13 Mechanical* and *The Death of the Pterodactyl*.

To begin with, he was content to glance at me over his newspaper, looking just long enough to make the message clear, but not so much that I was uncomfortable, and to put just a little too much intensity in his voice when he answered my banal questions (What kind of bread? Do you want it toasted? Swiss or cheddar? etc.). Then, one day, he gathered up all his courage and, with the brazenness of the very timid, broke the ice and initiated a conversation (or, more accurately, a soliloquy) comprising mainly of nervous laughter and poorly disguised bragging. Knowing himself to be entirely devoid of personal charm, he essentially tried to pick me up by bombarding me with his talents as a doctor and writer. He stopped just short of coming right out with, "I write books, do you want to sleep with me?"

I don't know what you think, but I don't reckon it's really the done thing to give your own book to someone. It's borderline rude. If you write songs or paint, you can always say, "Come on, I'll show you my painting," and even if your song's terrible or your picture's dreadful, it's no big deal, you've only wasted a few minutes of your victim's time. But reading a book takes much longer, and surely you'd have to be pathologically self-obsessed to ask someone to spend four or five hours of their life in your interior universe. At least Sébastien's books are short. That's what I told myself as I thanked him for his kind thought. In sixty minutes, stopwatch in hand, I could be all done and dusted with my suitor's literary output. "You don't have to read it, you know..." he said with forced indifference. But you only had to look at him to see that he would be suspended in unbearable uncertainty until I'd reassured him of his genius.

And what exactly is this meatball-sub-loving writer's prose like? How can I explain it? Let's just say, to keep things brief, it's exactly what you'd expect from a guy who wrote a thesis on the poetics of perception in Paul Valéry. It's nothing like Agatha Christie, if that's what you're thinking. In fact, it's not even anything like Alain Robbe-Grillet. Next to Sébastien Daoust, Samuel Beckett is a total lightweight and James Joyce looks like Patricia MacDonald. *The Death of the Pterodactyl* comes to just 146 pages. Taking into account the blank spaces at the ends of chapters and the fact that the work proper doesn't start until page seven, it wasn't asking the impossible. But still it dragged. To give you some idea, here's a brief extract, which I've copied word for word:

```
We were at Jim's, and Jim was talking to me about
antimatter. We were in the purple living room.
Jim claimed that it would have made no difference
if our universe had been made from antimatter. I
was having trouble following the conversation, so
absorbed was I in gazing at the walls. Why had
Jim chosen such an ugly colour for this room? "But
then," I threw out randomly, "could it be that the
universe actually is made of antimatter and we just
```

don't know it?" Jim said no, everything around us is matter because we have decided it is so. It's just a matter of convention. "So you're saying that if our universe was made of antimatter, we would call antimatter matter and vice versa." Jim replied that that was it exactly. So one fine morning Jim had gone into a paint shop and chosen, from among the millions of available shades, this purple. How strange. "Since we systematically designate every-thing around us by the word matter, surely that's the same as saying that antimatter can't exist." Jim was going to reply, but was stopped mid-flow by the doorbell. We sat in silence for a long minute, sipping our drinks. The doorbell rang again. "You should go and answer it," Jim said to me.

"Why me?"

"If it's someone selling something, they'll want to speak to the master of the house. And since we're at your house…"

That seemed logical to me. I got up and went to open the door. It was Quentin. He seemed amazed to see me. "Hello, Quentin. Jim and I have been waiting for you in the purple living room." I helped him off with his coat, all the while wondering why he'd rung the doorbell at his own house. But people have their little ways.

This was page thirty-four of *The Death of the Pterodactyl*, but that's really neither here nor there, given how much you could mix up the pages without affecting the work's comprehensibility in the slightest. In it, there is no sign whatsoever of what my guru (Marc Fisher) calls a "narrative arc." Worse still, there isn't even the tiniest reference to a pterodactyl. Of course, the next day, once he'd finished working with his boats, he came up to my counter in a tizzy. I pretended not to notice his questioning looks as I prepared his feast. After all, there was no reason I should have read his books already; surely he could give me a few days' grace. I was hoping another customer would show up, but, as I mentioned earlier, we weren't the busiest franchise in the chain (to the extent that we wondered, every month-end, how we were going to make ends meet).

"Well?" he asked at last, as I was giving him his change.

"Well what?"

"Well... have you had time to start my books?"

"Oh! Yes. And I've finished them too."

"And?"

The previous evening I'd gone to bed with the firm intention of telling him the truth, which would go something like: "Listen, Seb, I'm sure your books are as good as the guy who reviews for *OVNI* claims. First off, who am I to dig my heels in against an *OVNI* reviewer? It's just not really my cup of tea. And you must have noticed it's not really anyone's cup of tea when you got your royalty cheque, right?" But when you're a hypocrite like me, your firm resolve to tell the truth quickly flies out the window. And, anyway, what right do I have to wreck his day? He's just made it through eight hours of hard slog making fibreglass hulls and now he just wants to enjoy his juicy foot-long while reading Richard Martineau's column, after being assured by the girl of his dreams that he totally crushed Kafka. I'm not claiming to be kindness incarnate, but neither am I a superbitch. So I bullshitted. And since I was bullshitting, I wasn't going to do it by halves. I told him about his virtuosity, his daring; once I got going, I bandied about the names of Broch, Gombrowicz, Buzzati, Zeno of Elea (uttered for the first time in that Subway, no doubt). I'm pretty good at knowing what people want to hear; it's a kind of gift. Just for good measure, I finished up with a couple of flaws, clearly attributable to the limits of my own mind and to the gaps in my education. I listened to myself talk and I almost managed to convince myself that I *had* liked his books, forgetting that I'd skimmed them while watching *Ghost Hunters* on TV. Say what you like, but I offer a damn good service for nine forty-five an hour.

However, after he left, I thought it over again and wondered if maybe I'd overdone it a bit. I mean, he already had a crush on me, but now he'd be imagining that I was sensitive to his art, which might make him so obsessed with me that I'd never know a moment's peace again. Perhaps he'd start waiting for me after work, asking me out, constantly begging me to go back to his place, that kind of thing. What would I do then? Quit? Tell him straight, "I lied, I don't know what got into me, your books are as boring as watching Living Faith Television, and anyway I don't even know who Zeno of Elea was, I just pulled it out of the air"? I didn't need to resort to such extreme solutions. The following day, as soon as I set foot in the restaurant, Annick—the girl who opens—told me I'd received a letter "with no stamp on it." In fact, the only thing on the envelope was my name. When Annick undid the bundle of newspapers, she'd found it slipped between two copies of the *Journal de Montréal*. It must have been put there between the paperboy coming round and the restaurant opening, and I must admit that I, the world's laziest person, found it very sweet that someone would get up early for me. The missive went like this:

Tess,
I think I won't come here to eat anymore. It's a shame—your subs aren't bad, it's affordable, and it's really close to where I live. But I'm in love with you and I think it's a pretty safe bet that you don't feel the same way. To carry on seeing you

day after day would only make me suffer needlessly, and I've long since passed the age when needless suffering seems entertaining. I hope I'll be able to forget you quickly. However, if for one reason or another you would prefer me not to forget you, you can contact me at this address and this number: (…) But I don't think you will, so I bid you adieu. Sébastien

He kept his word and never again set foot on our premises. (And I'd be fired on the spot if my boss found out I'd driven away one of our only regular customers.) As far as I was concerned, he was right: I had no desire to tell him not to forget me. If it hadn't been for this Idea of the Century necessitating his participation (passive but crucial), there's a strong chance he'd already have done so. Instead, I worry I've reignited the flame. I do feel a bit guilty, but it was an exceptional situation. In any case, he would have all the time he needed to forget me for good once I'd made it to Bird-in-Hand.

✗···11···✗

THE IDEA OF THE CENTURY

(Part One)

So we were brainstorming, churning out crappy ideas and dodgy plans at top speed, when the neighbour, who's always around when it's time to poke his big nose into our business, just came out with, "I've got it, man: you can fund the trip by writing about it in a newspaper or magazine. Bruno Blanchet's been travelling the world for ten years, paying for his plane tickets by writing a weekly column in *La Presse...*"

I didn't pick up on it right away—we never really listen when the neighbour speaks—but, more out of despair than anything else, I pondered his idea for a few seconds during a brief silence, and I had to admit that it was worth looking into. It killed me to say this unlikely sentence: "Jude, I think this imbecile has said something not entirely stupid."

Neighbour: Which imbecile?

Jude: What did he say?

Me: This idea of selling the story of our trip to a magazine.

Jude: You think *National Geographic* is going to roll out the red carpet? You think they might buy a big story on rural Pennsylvania from two nobodies?

Neighbour: But Bruno Blanchet—

Jude: People have heard of Bruno Blanchet.

Neighbour: Not that many.

Jude: We'd have a better chance of writing a book. Publishing houses take on first-time authors.

Me: Well… maybe, but two significant obstacles come to mind.

Jude: And they are?

Me: Well, first of all, I can't help thinking we're putting the cart before the horse. To submit the tale of our trip to a publisher, we've got to write it first, and for that we need—ideally—to have made the trip. But the whole reason we need the money is to go on the trip.

Jude: We could ask for an advance.

Me: Yes, that's true—we just show up in the office of the boss of—I don't know—Québec Amérique, and say, "Hello, we're Tess and Jude. We'd like to go to Pennsylvania, but we're completely broke. You seem like a swell guy, salt of the earth, how about giving us a cheque for $15,000 for the rights to the book we plan to write when we get back? Who knows, with a bit of luck you might even sell two hundred copies."

Jude: Ye-es, when you put it like that… And what's the second obstacle?

Me: Nobody publishes travel writing anymore.

✕ ··· **12** ··· ✕

A DYING GENRE

Back in the day, people didn't have much leisure time and almost always travelled for a specific purpose, usually commercial or military. Thus, until the Renaissance, travel writing told the stories of military campaigns (Caesar's *Gallic Wars*, for example) or "business travel" (Marco Polo and his *Book of the Marvels of the World*). Petrarch was probably the first, in 1336, to put into a book the story of a purely touristy trip with the tale of his climb of Mount Ventoux. It was only a century later that travel literature really took off, thanks to two unrelated facts: the invention of the printing press, which democratized the book, and the discovery of the New World. Cortés's *Cartas de relación* from Mexico, and later the tales told by Cook, Bougainville, and La Pérouse about round-the-world voyages, would become real bestsellers. In the eighteenth and nineteenth centuries, the biggest authors tackled this multifaceted genre (which could take the form of essay, travel notebook, ethnographic study, autobiography, political analysis, or a simple collection of anecdotes), a sure sign that it had made it big. Among the best known, we could mention Laurence Sterne's *A Sentimental Journey through France and Italy*, Diderot's *Journey to Holland*, Chateaubriand's *Record of a Journey from Paris to Jerusalem*, Stendhal's *Memoirs of a Tourist*,

Over Strand and Field by Flaubert and Maxime Du Camp, as well as the very famous *Democracy in America* by Tocqueville. There were also a few dazzling successes in the first half of the twentieth century (Lévi-Strauss's *Tristes Tropiques*), but the genre declined rapidly after that. Progress in transportation and communication made travel banal. Today anyone can go anywhere or, failing that, anyone can chat about what's going on in Rio de Janeiro or Fort Myers, and anyone can learn, should they be interested, that Parrish Jason Casebier, of 2219 Florence Boulevard in Omaha, Nebraska, was convicted of "rape felony" on November 25, 1995.

x···13···x

THE IDEA OF THE CENTURY
(Continued and Concluded)

Jude: In that case, we just need to write "novel" on the cover and everyone will be fooled. People call anything a novel nowadays.

Me: That's true. But my first objection still stands: no publisher will agree to give a big advance to unknown authors. And we're not just unknown authors, we're not authors at all.

Jude: Huh! It's pretty easy to pick that up quickly, like everything else. But you're right. Publishers would go bust if they wrote cheques out to everyone who asked them nicely.

Me: Strike that idea then. Too bad. I really liked that one.

Neighbour: You could ask for a grant. The government gives artists tons of money. And then wonders why we're in the red...

It was at precisely that moment that I stopped thinking of the neighbour as a simple halfwit and saw him rather as one of those holy fools that proliferated in ancient Russia—those village idiots who were blessed once in a while with divine grace and could give great scholars a run for their money. In any case, just like the famous stopped clock, he'd just been right twice in the same day, which must be, beyond a shadow of a doubt, a personal record.

Jude: No, that wouldn't work.

Me: Why not?

Jude: Because the government only gives grants to established artists.

Me: Are you sure?

Jude: We can check the eligibility criteria to be sure, but I'm pretty much a hundred per cent certain.

Me: Fuck!

Neighbour: If you knew someone who wrote books, you could apply in their name…

Jude: A frontman…

We both caught on at the same instant. I started to protest, but not too strongly, and just for show, to square it with my conscience—which was, happily, not too difficult to satisfy.

Me: No, I can't ask him that.

Jude: Why not?

Me: He's trying to forget me. He might have forgotten me already.

Jude: I bet he hasn't.

Me: And besides…

Jude: Besides what?

Me: Besides, he cares about his reputation as a writer. They're vain, writers. Even when blinded by love, he'd never allow a book written by two amateurs to appear with his name on it.

Jude: Who's talking about appearing? That's the beautiful thing about government grants: you don't need to produce the final product. I expect we'll have to prove that we really wrote a book and tried to publish it, but I'd be amazed if they demanded the money back if we failed. We just churn out any old thing at top speed, and then send it to a publisher who doesn't focus on new talent. Boréal, for example. That way, we'll have a rejection letter as proof of our good faith.

Me: All right, maybe it does seem doable. In any case, it's the best thing we've come up with.

Jude: Doable? Come on, it's totally the idea of the century!

Neighbour: I preferred the idea of the massage parlour. Giving hand jobs seems less hassle than writing a book. I'd even advertise for you...

Me: Would you look at that—he's turned back into the village idiot again.

x ··· 14 ··· x

THE FRONTMAN

The first thing, before I went to talk to Sébastien, was to check that there was no other way of doing it. So I went on the Canada Council for the Arts website and the one for the Conseil des arts et des lettres du Québec, the two main governmental organizations to which artists can apply for a handout, so I could look over their eligibility criteria. Jude was right: you needed to be considered an artist before you could receive a single dollar from either organization. According to CALQ, the term *artist* is defined by four points. An artist is a person who:

1. *Calls him-/herself a professional artist.* (So far so good: "My name is Tess and I am a professional artist." First condition fulfilled, piece of cake.)
2. *Creates works or practises an art or offers services for payment, as a creator or an interpreter, particularly in the areas under the responsibility of the Conseil des arts et des lettres du Québec.* (Here, it's that "or" that saves me, because "practising an art" is basically meaningless. At a push, singing in the shower falls into that category. After two conditions, I'm still in the running, knock on wood.)
3. *Has peer recognition.* (Sure, and "peer" is defined as...)

4. *Publicly disseminates or interprets works in places and/or contexts recognized by his/her peers.* (Now it's getting trickier to play with the words. I don't think I've ever publicly disseminated anything. Shoot!)

As for the Canada Council for the Arts, they shut down all hope right from the start, stipulating that to be eligible for a grant you already need to have one published work. They put authors into three categories: emerging, for which you must have published one literary work and for which the maximum grant is $12,000; mid-career (two to five published works, maximum grant $25,000), and established (at least six published works, maximum grant $25,000). They apply the same distinctions to other art forms, even in the Aboriginal Dance Professional grant program. In case you're interested, a mid-career aboriginal dancer can apply for up to $25,000 for researching or developing a project.

Basically, we really were going to need a frontman. Luckily, I'd kept Sébastien's letter with his contact details. (It was, after all, the first—and would doubtless be the last—love letter I'd received.) I dithered a bit as to whether I should call or write, and ended up going with the latter. That would give him the option of not replying if he didn't want anything to do with it.

Sébastien,
I don't want to tell you how to run your own life, but it seems to me that you're going about things the wrong way if you want to get over this absurd infatuation with me. By staying away from me, you'll just start idealizing me, dreaming up a load of nonsense about me, inventing conversations between us before you fall asleep at night. And don't deny it: you artists are all good at that.

If you really want to know, the best way to get sick of me is to see me. Anyway, I think it would be worth a shot. What are you doing tomorrow evening? Do you fancy having a beer with me? Please don't reply: that way you can change your mind right up to the last minute. I'll be at Chez Véro from eight o'clock on.
Tess

I headed over to Chez Véro an hour early so I could down a beer before Sébastien turned up. I hadn't thought too much about how to bring up my request, but I could always start by asking him if he had something on the go. After all, *The Death of the Pterodactyl* had come out in 2006 (its eight readers would surely be getting impatient), and if he had an ongoing project for which he was intending to apply for a grant, our plan would be wrecked. He arrived right on time, I waved at him, and he came to join me at my table. He seemed flustered, which is probably what always happens when you see someone you've written a love letter to. At the best of times he wasn't exactly a relaxed sort of guy, but now he was completely pathetic. He avoided looking at me and picked at the label on his beer bottle to have something to focus on.

I pretended not to notice his unease, and kept the conversation going as best I could. "Have you been to Chez Véro before?"

"Um... no, I don't think so."

"The Vault Café is more your sort of thing..."

"Actually, I don't go out much. Sometimes I go with the guys from the shop to Chez Tonio."

"And you chat about the problem of time in Paul Valéry?"

"I can't say that's ever come up, no."

"So, which of our competitors did you betray us for?"

"Huh?"

"Where are you eating now that you're boycotting Subway?"

"Depends. At Auger most of the time."

"Good choice, but they don't serve subs there."

"This might surprise you, but I don't just eat subs."

"I suppose that's possible, you know, like that big bonehead in those old commercials."

"Jared?"

"I would never have remembered his name."

Our conversation struggled on like that for a good hour, neither of us daring to bring up the subject closest to our hearts. But I could see he was gathering up the courage to raise his, with each slug of beer bringing us closer to the moment he'd dare to start talking about his feelings. Wanting to avoid this at all costs, I knocked his legs out from under him by setting my cards out first.

"So, Seb, have you got a project on the go at the moment?"

"On the go?"

"I mean, are you working on a literary project?"

"No."

"Yeah, I know, authors never like talking about their writing."

"I'm not writing anything."

"You're not writing anymore?"

"No."

"Why?"

"Because I don't believe in it anymore."

"You don't believe in it?"

"That's right."

"But all that literature study—"

"You don't learn how to become a writer in a classroom, you know."

"Neither do you become a doctor of literature to make rowboats for minimum wage."

"We don't make rowboats at Doral, we make yachts and

cruisers. And I make fifteen bucks an hour."

"Oh, excuse *me*... And that was your plan, while you were studying, to come back to Grand-Mère to build cruisers?"

"No, I wanted to be a literature prof."

"What made you change your mind?"

"I don't believe in that anymore either."

"You and your beliefs, you are funny. How much does a university prof earn a year?"

"A hundred and twenty thousand at the top of the scale, something like that."

"So only three or four times what someone who makes rowboats—sorry, cruisers—earns. So do you believe in boats?"

"Yes, boats have a purpose."

"And literature?"

"Has none."

He'd stopped fiddling with the label on his Labatt's 50 and was looking at me defiantly. The conversation was becoming interesting, and in the normal run of things I would really enjoy taking him down a peg or two, but I had to keep my goal in mind, so I went off on a tangent and said to him, "I have a favour to ask you." He let out a sigh, barely perceptible, just so that I knew he wasn't surprised, that he hadn't really thought I was there for his good looks. "What sort of favour?"

"A literary service, naturally."

"You've got a paper to hand in and you want me to knock it into shape."

"No, nothing like that. It's ages since I set foot in a school, and anyway, without wanting to insult you, I'd never employ you as a 'knocker into shape.' Actually, it's just your name I need."

"My name? Why?"

"I think I should start at the beginning. To make a long story short, we want to go to Bird-in-Hand but we're broke, so we've been looking for a way to—"

"'We'? Who's 'we'?"

"Me and Jude. As I was saying, we want to go to Bird-in-Hand and—"

"Jude's your boyfriend?"

"What's that got to do with the story? Listen, I've got three pints in my system. I'm already having trouble collecting my thoughts; I'll never get to the end if you keep interrupting me every sentence."

"Just explain who Jude is and then I'll shut up."

"All right…how should I put this? In your letter you wrote that you were in love with me, right?"

"Um…well…yes…"

"Did you know that the human body is roughly eighty per cent water?"

"I don't follow you."

"Well, when we talk about 'Tess,' it's mostly a question of water. If you claim to be in love with me, it's mainly water that you love."

"That's an interesting way of looking at things. And rather stupid, if I may say so. But I'm really not following you."

"Let me spell it out: if you're in love with someone, you're in love with the whole person, not just a part of them. If you're in love with me, you're in love with my right ear, my chin, my nose. You can't say, 'I'm in love with Tess except for her nose.'"

"Obviously not. Anyway, your nose is fantastic."

"Oh, come off it! What I'm trying to get across is that Jude is just as much a part of me as my right ear, my nose, and my half-dozen gallons of water…"

"So I would be in love with Jude…"

"Um… Well, yes! That's right. Now can I ask you the favour?"

"Go ahead. I've just learned that I'm in love with some guy I didn't even know existed; after that I'm ready to hear anything."

"Here we go: Jude and I want to go to Bird-in-Hand—"

"Where's that?"

"In Pennsylvania, Lancaster County."

"Why do you want to go there?"

"To be totally honest, we don't really know why. My personal theory is that people want to get away when they're unhappy, but Jude claims we're too unimportant to be unhappy."

"Rubbish! Even dogs can be unhappy…"

"Well, yeah, but for a guy who promised he wouldn't interrupt anymore…"

"Sorry. I won't say another word."

"Right. Take eight. Jude and I want to go to Bird-in-Hand—for no good reason, we just want to—and, as I was saying, we're poor: I make subs and he doesn't do anything. We've been racking our brains to find some way of coming up with $15,000, but we're too lazy to make any great effort, too impatient to save, too cowardly to rob a bank, and too stupid to come up with a scam, so we've decided to turn to the government—"

"They already give money to lazy-asses, cowards, and scammers…"

"I'm not talking about welfare, I'm talking about a grant. A grant to support creation, to be precise."

"Literary creation?"

"Yes, we're going to write up our trip and submit it to publishers, but the problem is that to be eligible you need to have already published a book. You've published two—which, incidentally, makes you a mid-career writer—so I was wondering…"

"You want me to apply for a grant for you?"

"Not even that, we're organizing everything. We just need your permission to use your name. In fact, the only thing you'll need to do will be to cash the cheque and transfer the money to us."

"Has anyone ever told you you're a very strange girl?"

"Once or twice, yes. So what's your answer?"

"Well…yes, why not? On one condition: that you don't send your manuscript to my former publisher."

"No, that's fine. But otherwise you're really on board?"

"Yes, I don't care, if it helps you out…"

"Of course, we'll let you read our manuscript before we send it."

"There's no need."

"What! You wouldn't care if a book you hadn't even read was published with your name on the cover?"

"No, I think I'd find it funny. Anyway, they'll reject you."

"Yeah, Jude said we don't actually need to get to the publication stage to get the grant. But how can you be so sure ahead of time?"

"They reject just about everybody."

"Just about…"

"Publishers accept approximately one per cent of the manuscripts they receive in the mail. But like you say, that doesn't matter, since you're just doing it for the grant."

"No, it doesn't matter."

x···15···x

THERE'S NO ACCOUNTING FOR TASTE

He insisted on walking me home. I wasn't especially keen for him to know where I lived, but I couldn't work out how to say no. Before we said goodbye, he said, "Now that you've asked me your favour, I suppose I'll never see your face again."

"Oh, come on, we'll get together again. Whenever you like."

"Can I have your number?"

"I haven't got one, but I check my email all the time."

"All right. Goodnight."

"Goodnight."

Damn! Here was something I hadn't thought about: from now until the cash was in our hands, I was going to have to be nice to Sébastien. I didn't know how far being kind to him might stretch, but definitely not as far as he hoped. In fact, right then, I really wanted to strangle him. But why? He'd agreed to be our frontman without any fuss, he'd totally saved our lives. Under the circumstances, surely I could have summoned up a little gratitude. But no, I resented him. It's no use beating around the bush, I know perfectly well why I'm so annoyed: it was his "They'll reject you." He'd announced it as if it was a foregone conclusion, calmly, without any malice in his voice. A simple observation.

When he saw me come home in such a bad mood, Jude

immediately concluded that the plan had bombed, that we'd be forced to move on to our second-worst idea (selling a kidney on the black market?), so I immediately rushed to reassure him: no need to fret, everything was in hand, we could start filling in the application. There was just a little adjustment to the program. What kind of little adjustment? Just that the idea of scribbling down a manuscript and sending it any old where, fraudulent and chock full of errors, on the pretext that all we needed was a rejection letter proving that we really had submitted a literary work to a publisher, well, that wouldn't do, we'd have to make an effort (and at the word *effort,* I saw his face fall, but I didn't let myself be swayed) and we'd write a real book, a good book, or at least good enough to fall into the "one per cent accepted" category, and exactly one year from now we'd be on display in the local bookshop, I give you my word. He didn't grumble, he knew I wouldn't change my mind: like all people who have no backbone, I rarely make a decision, but on the rare occasions that I do, I will stick to it come hell or high water, even if it flies in the face of common sense.

That same evening we set out our game plan. Rather than simply telling the story of our trip, the narrative would also cover the preparation period, which meant we wouldn't have to wait until we'd come back from Bird-in-Hand to make a start on the task. I planned to get going with it the next day, and to write as much as I could think of, before handing the baton to Jude, who would give it back when he in turn ran out of inspiration. We would make the style and the formatting consistent during rewrites. And the very next day, after pottering around for a bit, I made myself a pot of tea, sat down in front of the computer, opened up Microsoft Word (which took it upon itself to call our work *Document 1,* but it won't stay like that), and I began to write down this story you're reading. Do you know what you call it when an author talks about the book she's writing in her book?

A mise-en-abyme. Truly there's a word for everything. (You can also write it as *abîme*, but it looks more stylish with the *y*.) As it happens I've learned a bit about the writing process and style these last couple of weeks. I even know what is a hyperbaton. And a hypotyposis. (That last full sentence contained a hyperbaton. Impressive, right?)

At the beginning, I didn't worry about such things, I just started muddling my way through, my only rule being to not piss off my reader (even though this reader was still a theoretical creature), writing something that I might want to read myself. I decided to divide my books into chapters of different lengths, each corresponding to one writing session. It was only at the end of the fourth of these sessions that I started to have doubts, to wonder if it had really been wise to appoint myself the judge. Being judge and defendant is never comfortable. I told myself that my personal tastes frequently matched up with those of publishing professionals, since all the good books I'd read had previously been accepted by a publisher. Yes, but so had the bad ones. To take an example close at hand: if I'd been on the editorial board and *13 Mechanical* or *The Death of the Pterodactyl* had landed on my desk, would I have given them the green light? Not on your life! I'd have shouted, "This is such a mess! I can't make head nor tail of it!" and I'd have moved on to the next one in the pile. And let's be honest, I've not exactly read tons of Québécois books this past year. So how would I know what today's publishers mean by a good manuscript?

So I went to find out right from the source. Credit where credit is due, I started by searching the Éditions du Boréal website (www.editionsboreal.qc.ca). On the home page there are links to "Current Titles" and "Recent Releases," as well as a series of scrolling menus giving access to different sections ("History," "Our Team," "Collections," "Events," "Prizes and Honours," "Catalogue," "Our Authors," and so on), but nothing about the kind of manuscripts they were looking for. It was only after a good bit of trial and error that I finally unearthed a short paragraph in the FAQs: "If you want to send us your manuscript (all fiction— including crime—and essays[1]), you can either deliver it in person to our offices or send it by courier (we only accept hard-copy manuscripts—no disks or email attachments). In either case we will acknowledge receipt and send your manuscript on to the editorial board for evaluation. Please do not send originals." At Québec Amérique (www.quebec-amerique.com), they are slightly more welcoming to budding authors. First of all, there's a link on the home page to a section called "Manuscripts," and they kindly take the time to explain exactly why they'll most likely reject us: "Last year Québec Amérique received, across all categories, some 800 manuscripts and proposals. (...) When we point out that barely four per cent of these proposals will make it to publication, it is perhaps unnecessary to emphasize how important it is for authors to give themselves every chance." There are several recommendations regarding the presentation of manuscripts (no electronic formats, print on one side only, sensible line spacing, etc.) but, once again, nothing about the literary qualities they're looking for. Same goes for VLB, who want pages to be numbered but not joined, printed on one side only, on 8.5 by 11 paper, and, they add sententiously, "Any manuscript not respecting these instructions will be automatically rejected and destroyed." As far as their preferred genres go, they stick to the same line as their colleagues at Boréal: "The Ville-Marie Littérature Group publishes mainly novels, poetry, essays, reportage, as well as short stories and biographies of famous people." Well, geez, surely that's pretty obvious: what

---

[1] "Boréal does not accept manuscripts in the following genres: poetry, plays, science-fiction or fantasy novels, or practical or esoteric books." No science fiction, noted. But what else?

kind of fool would write a biography of some unknown person? Over at Marchand de Feuilles (www.marchanddefeuilles.com), they're much more easygoing. Not a word about pagination and line spacing, and they even accept manuscripts by email. What's more, they're open to discovery: "Marchand de Feuilles is always on the lookout for new authors and illustrators. Our company is open to all innovative projects." Bring it on! They finish off with a cheerful, "Looking forward to reading your work!" Okay, so it's not particularly illuminating, but it's certainly welcoming. At HMH (www.editionshurtubise.com), they have more or less the same basic demands as the others with regard to format, but are equally quiet on the subject of content. (However, if you go to the trouble of studying their catalogue, you'll note that they have something of a weakness for retired French teachers churning out eighteen-volume historical sagas.)

Let's have a look at the Quebec City publishers now. At Septentrion (www.septentrion.qc.ca), they're pretty hardcore: under the section "Submit a Manuscript," there's a link to a six-page PDF detailing all their desiderata, of which a few examples: "Do not justify the text"; "buzzwords and neologisms should be enclosed in French quotation marks (e.g., <<alternative>>)"; "Use page breaks rather than a string of carriage returns"; "When a citation is preceded by a colon, the main sentence should still be punctuated even if the quotation itself finished with an ellipsis, an exclamation mark, or a question mark"; "It's important to properly distinguish between natural features and official place names"; "Do not insert images into the text, but mark the illustration number at the relevant point"; etc. I wonder if they've ever received a single passable manuscript. At L'Instant Même (www.instantmeme.com), they're much less strict, but they still don't want to be sent just any old thing. For example, they won't accept anything shorter than a hundred pages, which is, they specify, about 184,000 characters, including spaces. (That shouldn't be any trouble for me: I'm already at 112,000!) Alto (www.edition-salto.com) doesn't ask for the moon on a stick either: they want bound manuscripts, carefully presented, and accompanied, if possible, by a brief synopsis of the work. In addition, following the example of Marchand de Feuilles, they accept manuscripts electronically. (Speaking of which: Les Intouchables [www.lesintouchables.com] want nothing to do with paper; they expect to receive manuscripts by email, in the interests of saving trees. If you want to know my opinion, I'd say they've managed to find other ways of polluting.)

x···16···x

MY OWN YODA

In short, every publisher has their own preferences about how the manuscripts they receive should be presented, but as far as content goes, they leave that entirely to our discretion. (If I was a publisher, though, I can't help thinking I'd be tempted to say: "Present it any way you like, as long as it's legible, you can even write it in ballpoint pen if your handwriting's decent, but please be advised that any manuscript relating the adventures of a thirtysomething drowning his romantic sorrows in some bar in Plateau-Mont-Royal will be shredded on sight.") From this I concluded that if I wanted to get some tips on how to appeal to editorial boards, I was going to have to find myself a mentor, someone who knew his stuff, who could do for me what Mr. Miyagi did for Daniel, what Apollo did for Rocky, or Yoda for Luke Skywalker. When I talked to Jude about it, he replied that it wasn't a very difficult choice because the only published author I knew was Sébastien, but seriously, I'd rather die than ask him for advice. I had no desire to give him a chance to pontificate, and above all I didn't want to tip him off about my ambitions. In any case, his instruction would be useless to me, since I had no intention of writing experimental shit. So I turned instead to everyone's favourite mentor, Google, and asked it straight out,

"How do you get published?" The first three or four pages of results linked to articles in French magazines, to self-publishing sites, and to forums where total unknowns give infallible tips on how to become a successful author. It was only around the fifth page that the vaguely familiar name of Marc Fisher showed up for the first time, as Amazon was promoting his book *The Work of the Novelist followed by Advice on Getting Published and The Art of Suspense in Mary Higgins Clark*. All I knew at that point about Marc Fisher was that he was part of a select club of Quebec writers living by their pens, and that around the turn of the millennium he'd made it big with a little philosophical novel called *The Millionaire*—which had been translated into several languages and had sold well in the US—and that since then he'd been shamelessly repackaging the same material in multiple sequels. I didn't know, however, that he'd fallen as low as literary theory. The blurb read as follows: "The novelist's job has always fascinated people. In this little work bursting with relevant observations, Marc Fisher relates the highs and the lows, revealing what awaits new writers. He also gives, with the practical wisdom that can only come from experience, valuable pointers to the beginner novelist in search of a publisher as well as the published novelist in search of…readers. Along the way, he humorously relates all the difficulties he encountered before managing to get his books published abroad (they've been trans-lated into more than twenty-five languages) and explains how he snagged an international agent. Finally, in a marvellous little work, he analyzes the narrative processes of the contemporary queen of suspense, Mary Higgins Clark. The three short essays in this book together make up a veritable goldmine of reflections and recommendations that will be as useful to the budding nov-elist as they are to a writer who is already published and dreams of living by his or her pen."

Something told me I'd just found my Yoda. That same evening, I went to the Hélène-B.-Beauséjour library to borrow *The Work of the Novelist*. I also noted that Mr. Fisher had published, several years earlier, another book on the same subject, *Letter to a Young Novelist*. Cynics will not fail to note the many similarities between these two works, going as far as to say that the second is, for all intents and purposes, a warmed-over version of the first. But that's true only at the level of content. The covers aren't at all similar—the cover of *Advice to a Young Novelist* (published by Québec Amérique) is brown, while that of *The Work of the Novelist* (Trait d'union) is a lovely azure blue. And, while we're splitting hairs, it is actually possible to find differences between the two texts. For example, in *Advice*, Mr. Fisher talks at greater length about writing techniques (which is why I took it for my main reference source), while in *Work*, he spends more time telling the story of his own professional journey, and I'm really tempted to summarize the whole thing right here. But that would be yet another digression, and my master doesn't like digressions. Here's what he has to say, among other things, on the subject: "Pedal to the metal. You must live in step with your era, which is, whether you like it or not, one of speed. Proust, brilliant as he was, would effectively be impossible today, with his half-page sentences, his endless analyses. (…) Avoid overly long descriptions, which are tedious in any case, and which the impatient reader sees as a chore that he or she would happily skip, despite your sparkling style. (…) Yes, put the pedal to the metal, like a driver drunk on speed" (*Advice to a Young Novelist*, page 104). But I dare to think he might forgive me, just this once, for taking the scenic route, especially if I'm talking about him. Anyway, there'll be time for pruning at the rewriting stage. So, here's how this modern-day Lucien de Rubempré started his literary career.

The first thing you need to know is that Marc Fisher didn't start off as Marc Fisher, but as plain old Marc-André Poissant, which, let's be honest, is not the most successful name you can imagine. Destined by his upbringing for a liberal profession, he started a law degree without really thinking about it, but he'd known ever since his late teenage years that he'd never become a lawyer. Music was his first love. He learned classical guitar and even auditioned for the Montreal Conservatory, although he didn't get in. Next he turned to chess, but although he had a certain amount of talent, he was sensible enough to know that chess as a career could only work for a few hundred people in the entire world. The career of novelist soon came to mind and, with the beautiful innocence of youth, he launched himself headlong into it, spending two years working on a novel entitled *Silène*. As soon as he'd written the final period, he hired someone to type it up and sent it to Cercle du Livre de France, a fashionable publisher at the time. A few weeks later he received a rejection letter. He was, of course, disappointed by this, but didn't let himself get discouraged and sent his manuscript to a different publisher. This last, a relation of his father, agreed to meet him to explain the editorial board's decision. However, face to face or by letter, the result was the same: the publisher declared the work to be unpublishable and its author completely devoid of talent. "I have no advice to give you," the editor said, "but I'm going to be like everyone else and give you some anyway... What I'm about to say might seem harsh, but with time you'll come to see that I'm right... You can stick with it, of course... But in my opinion—and I've seen a lot of young people come along before you—you're wasting your time... You haven't got what it takes to become a novelist" (*The Work of the Novelist*, page 26). Fortunately Mr Fisher was gracious enough not to name this editor. Imagine what an idiot he must feel today!

Did Marc-André Poissant let himself get knocked down by these disappointments? Absolutely not! He set to work once again and started to write what would become his first published novel: *Paul Desormeaux, Student*. In the intervening time, since he also had to live, he found work as an editor at a publishing house. His employers, aware of his abilities as a writer, set him a thankless task: writing the "autobiography" of a recovering alcoholic singer (whom he once again declined to name). This little work, written in around sixty hours, sold no fewer than forty thousand copies. A bestseller! This great success had the happy effect of putting him in his employer's good books; to compensate him, they agreed to give him a chance and publish *Paul Desormeaux, Student*. And, as if that wasn't enough, the novelist Marie-Claire Blais, who'd just won the prestigious Medici Prize for *A Season in the Life of Emmanuel*, agreed to recommend the novel, which appeared with the blurb "We are witnessing the birth of a great writer." (I like to imagine Ms. Blais bringing it up every time she gets tipsy: "I don't like to boast, dear friends, but I actually played a part in discovering Marc Fisher...")

The book sold seven thousand copies, which is very respectable, especially for a debut. (I would be astonished if more than seventy copies of *The Death of the Pterodactyl* had sold.) But rather than resting on his laurels and staying in his comfort zone, Marc-André decided to switch genres and write a suspense novel (*The Mirror of Folly*), in which a young woman neglected by her husband claims to receive anonymous phone calls and threatening letters, of which she herself is actually the author. Caught in her own trap, she soon ends up in a lunatic asylum. (Note to self: Ask the lady at Hélène-B.-Beauséjour to order it.) This time, sales rose to thirteen thousand copies. However, despite this success, Marc-André was still not satisfied. He knew he hadn't yet found his voice, his own style. Incidentally, his next two novels were failures. In hindsight, he recognized that his first novels had had considerable problems, and so it was to help his readers avoid making the same mistakes that he wrote his two short treatises on narratology.

But how did Marc-André Poissant, a young and inexperienced author, become the demigod of letters known as Marc Fisher? Here's his answer: "I've been through many different kinds of suffering, interior experiences (…) that have radically changed me, my powers of concentration, my sensitivity, and have made me the person I've always dreamed of becoming, this novelist that I was not, and would never have become, without this mysterious transformation" (*The Work of the Novelist*, page 30). Is there more? What exactly were these different kinds of sufferings, these interior experiences? Mr Fisher draws a discreet veil over this aspect of his life. (A veil that he does, however, lift in his book *The Soul's Ascent* [Un Monde Différent Editions], available at all good bookshops.) For the time being, all he tells us is that it was the start of the real journey. "Yes, in the end lead does turn into gold, just as the water was changed into wine at the wedding at Cana (…)." At the end of this transformation, he had several more years of fumbling around, during which he was, by turns, acquisitions editor, writer, and slave once more. And then, at the age of thirty-four, he wrote *The Millionaire*. The rest you know.

✗···**17**···✗

LESSONS FROM THE MASTER

Marc Fisher's teachings consist mainly of practical tips, stuff you can immediately put to use. He's not the type to get overly bothered about the characters' arcs and interactions, and there's no way you'll ever see him getting bogged down in the distinction between a heterodiegetic and a homodiegetic narrator. He's keener on the famous "show don't tell," beloved of Anglo-Saxon writers (rather than simply saying that Lisette is jealous, show her losing her mind with jealousy), and on narrative consistency (if you learn, in the first chapter, that Lisette is a jealous woman, don't forget to make her act accordingly for the rest of the book). "How do you get published?" he asks in *Advice on Getting Published.* "Write a good novel!" he shoots back. "Editors are like bees: give them a successful manuscript whose every page is a perfumed petal, enthralling, profound, and beautiful, and they will absolutely have to interrupt their busy flight to publish you" (*The Work of the Novelist*, page 79). It's nicely put, right? The whole thing's like this from start to finish.

He scorns a whole swath of "literary romantics" who don't believe that a novel should bend to any rule, that it should "simply emerge, magnificent and perfect, from the dishevelled head of its genius creator." Inspiration is good, he's not going to argue with that, but let's not forget that Bach and Mozart had teachers, and that Picasso and Rodin studied fine arts, and so on. What was good for them should certainly be good for you, should it not? That said, he devotes his first chapter to the problem of character, because this, according to him, is where debut novelists make the most blunders. Well, as far as we're concerned, our hands are somewhat tied since we are the characters. You do what you can with what you have, right? So I'll skip to the next chapter, in which Marc lists what he likes to call the ten great qualities of a novel. In his opinion, "the more you inject these qualities into your novel, the more happiness you'll produce in your future reader and the greater your chance of being published" (*The Work of the Novelist*, page 113). Let's quickly look them over, just so I can see how I've been doing so far.

Quality 1: *Emotion*. That this quality comes first is not an accident, since "a good novel is above all an *emotional experience*, not an intellectual one. And remember that if your characters' fate doesn't move you, there's a high likelihood that the reader will be indifferent too" (*The Work of the Novelist*, page 114). Um…does my fate interest you, dear reader? No, no, please don't answer out loud.

Quality 2: *Relatability*. "Novels that have characters in which everyone can recognize themselves generally do well." There's no point burying my head in the sand here: I'm off to a bad start. The good news is that there are still eight qualities to turn things around.

Quality 3: *Suspense*. "Suspense means tight, fast-paced writing with minimal exposition; it's light on description and psychological analysis, and has frequent but not chatty dialogue, and above all, a large number of narrative units, which means, basically, events. When there's not much going on, you lose attention" (*The Work of the Novelist*, page 115). Microsoft Word confirms that my file will soon hit twenty-three thousand words and apparently I'm still setting the scene: so much for "minimal exposition." On the other hand, you have to admit it's pretty low-key on the descriptions and psychological analysis fronts. As for these pesky narrative units, I can only repeat that we do what we can with what we have. Fewer things have happened in our entire lives than in a single Dan Brown paragraph. I can't bring myself to believe that things happen to us for the sole purpose of stopping our attention from wandering.

Quality 4: *Humour.* "Clearly, being funny—particularly on command—isn't easy, and it's probably a gift, something that can't easily be taught. (…) For us mere mortals, being funny on command is an unreasonable demand" (*The Work of the Novelist,* pages 115–16). Do you find me funny, reader? Personally, I can't really tell. I mean, Jude and I are a good audience for each other, but we rarely get the chance to test our material on other people. Annick at Subway seems to find me hilarious, but she's always sniggering anyway. Plus, I've noticed that she finds me funniest when I'm not trying to be funny. Anyway, it's difficult to play the clown for a reader who's still theoretical. Not being acquainted with you personally, I don't know if Lise Dion or Groucho Marx gets you going, or Marcel Gamache or Molière. To deal with all contingencies, I'm inserting a joke here that will, I'm sure, be universally appreciated. Then at least you'll have got one laugh out of this story.

Two ducks are chatting beside a pond.
"Quack quack!" says one.
And the other replies:
"I was just about to say the same thing!"

Quality 5: *Romanticism.* "A novel in which men and women hang out together for two hundred pages without the slightest amorous spark flying seems artificial, cold, and lacking" (*The*

Work of the Novelist, page 116). Once again, I'll just say in my defence that the material I'm working with is not especially fruitful in this respect. If we disregard those who are only mentioned in passing (such as my colleague Annick, about whom I was just talking), this story would have just three characters: 1. Jude and me; 2. Sébastien Daoust; 3. the neighbour (and even that's barely more than a walk-on part). We're certainly not going to start something with the neighbour just so you can get your dose of romance. (Bleurgh! Just thinking about it gives me the hee-bie-jeebies.) Look, I'd rather fall in love with an inanimate object than with the neighbour. That's a thing, you know. I read in the paper the other day about some guy in Australia who developed a crazy passion for an umbrella, not just sexual attraction, like a fetish, but an actual romantic attachment. There's even a name for it, but I forget what. When they say it takes all sorts, they aren't joking. Here's a few more: do you know what dendrophilia is? Sexual attraction to trees. Exobiophilia? That's when you have a thing for aliens. If you're an asthenophile, you get turned on by being ill, if you are an emetophile, by vomit, and you can be sure that if someone's gone to the trouble of inventing the words it's because they're real things. People look all innocent when you pass them in the street, but there are all kinds of lunatics out there. But now I'm getting sidetracked again.

Quality 6: *Information*. "Every time your novel teaches the reader something about other countries, other cultures, times or places that he doesn't know, or doesn't know very well, you score points. Who doesn't want to learn while they're enjoying themselves?" So you have nothing to complain about. I bet that two minutes ago you didn't know what emetophilia was. It might not be the kind of word you'll manage to insert into conversation all that often, but it's better to know too much than too little, right?

Quality 7: *Imagination*. "(…) to spice up a dull scene, set it in an unexpected location. For example, take that business meeting in the predictable conference room and set it in a Jacuzzi or at the top of a mountain. An amorous encounter taking place in a bar, like so many others? Go right now and set it in an ambulance (…)" (*The Work of the Novelist*, page 119). I honestly don't think I have any imagination. When I was little I got myself out of trouble (behaving badly, not doing my homework, etc.) with a repertoire of three or four lies, which I served up to my parents, my teachers, my conscience whenever required. However, unless I'm very much mistaken, the present "novel" is probably the first to relate a journey to Bird-in-Hand. That's at least as original as a business meeting in a Jacuzzi.

Quality 8: *Structure*. "When your work is structured well, when nothing is superfluous, the publisher can tell, and that will make him or her favourable toward you" (*The Work of the Novelist*, page 120). Not applicable to the present situation: this being a travel narrative, it would be difficult to fit it into a framework.

Quality 9: *Philosophy*. "Works that make us think stay with us longer because they provoke stirrings deep inside us that alter us; it's as if they're talking about us and, above all, about what we could become" (*The Work of the Novelist*, page 121). I'm realistic enough to know, dear reader, that by this point it's been a good while since you've relied on me to explain the meaning of everything to you. However, at college I got unbelievably good marks in philosophy, but I must confess it takes a complete idiot to not get good marks. I remember spending ages on syllogisms ("All mice like cheese; Bobby likes cheese. What can we deduce? a) that Bobby is a mouse; b) that Bobby is not a mouse; c) that Bobby might or might not be a mouse.") and on the biographies of some important philosophers (Socrates was as ugly as sin, Spinoza's dad made spectacles, Nietzsche died in an asylum, Schopenhauer left all his worldly goods to his poodle, etc.). We also had to puzzle over boring ethical dilemmas (A boat is sinking; there are twenty people on board but the lifeboat has room for only ten. What criteria do you use to allocate the spaces?). Basically, the really important questions went unmentioned, and in any case, I reckon my teacher at the time was, despite his PhD, as clueless as his own cleaning lady about the great mysteries of life. Which means it was all very well frittering our time away on stories about mice who like cheese, but now I'm completely powerless to soothe your metaphysical anguish. Remember, though, that it was me who suggested you read *Livre M* by Paule Doyon, in which *everything* is explained. You could certainly call that a shot on goal.

Quality 10: *Style*. "Between a somewhat clumsy storyteller and an impeccable stylist with nothing to say, the ordinary reader will always choose the former, whose weaknesses will quickly be forgotten as he or she enjoys being caught up in the story" (*The Work of the Novelist*, page 124). Reading these two treatises, you quickly work out that style is Marc Fisher's pet peeve. He holds back—with a great deal of difficulty—from advising his disciples to write like pigs, but he never misses a chance to mock stylists. He contrasts, for example, the Goncourts, those upholders of "artistic style," with Zola and Balzac, whose slick writing was free of superfluous ornamentation, noting in passing that nobody reads the Goncourts anymore and that their name would have been forgotten if Edmond had not had the felicitous idea of founding a literary prize. In fact, he simply recommends not wasting too much time on it, because the "the public pays no heed to style. Yes, they want a certain level of accuracy, but apart from that they really only care about the story." And he carries on with his sledgehammer argument: to have any hope of living by one's pen, a Quebec writer has to target the international market, and that style can't survive translation. Under such conditions, the best thing is to aim for an "invisible" style, which fades into the background to allow the characters and events to take centre stage. He quotes the case of the English translation of *Madame*

Bovary, in which "nothing remains of the master's inimitable style, of his deep and sonorous phrasing." What a fool old Gustave was, to have gone to so much trouble! What's the good of all that effort if you're still going to go unnoticed by the Americans?

✖ ··· **18** ··· ✖

SPELLING MISTAKE COOKIES

This list of the ten crucial qualities of novels represents just a tiny part of Marc Fisher's teachings, but at least it gives you some idea of how far I've got to go. I won't despair though. At worst, everything I've done so far will have been good training, improving my skills. I can easily delete everything and start again with a blank slate, and you need never know anything about it. Anyway, we'll see.

Of all the precepts the master tries to inculcate in his padawan (put down the *OED*, it won't be in there, try Wikipedia instead), the one he comes back to the most could be formulated thus: "Strike early and strike often!" Modern readers, the former Mr. Poissant tells us, often judge a work on its first chapter, or even its first page or first line. The publisher is no exception. And what strikes their eyes first? The title, of course. This is why the importance of the title can't be overstated. "In some ways this is your window. What makes a good title? There are no hard and fast rules. Generally, go with short titles over long ones, but there are notable exceptions" (*The Work of the Novelist*, page 130). So that doesn't help me much, but in any case, I've never really liked someone else doing my dirty work. (I'd never dare repeat that last sentence if I was hooked up to a lie detector.) After reading these lines, I dog-eared the page and called Jude to drop everything and come and join me in the living room (it was good timing: he was doing precisely nothing), for one of those brainstorming sessions we were so good at.

"We need a title," I announced.

"Okay, I'd like to be a duke."

"Stop playing the fool, I mean a title for our book."

"Oh. I thought you'd already come up with one."

"No, it's called *Document 1* for now, but that's what Microsoft Word thought of. Surely we can do better."

"There's no hurry."

"True, but if we always put things off until the next day, it'll still be called *Document 1* by the time we're ready to send it out."

"And your sister will accuse us of procrastinating again."

"She said we were vacillatory, but I have to admit it more or less comes to the same thing. So, any ideas?"

"Um…we could ask Dany Laferrière. He's a pro at titles."

"Yeah, *I Am a Japanese Writer* and *How to Make Love to a Negro Without Getting Tired* are supercool. But I bet he keeps them all for himself; those writing types are always arrogant. And surely we can come up with something ourselves."

"Do you have an idea then?"

"What do you think of *Spelling Mistake Cookies*?"

"What does that mean?"

"Nothing. It's a dream I had. I was at my mother's, but not where she lives now, more like our house on Seventh, but it wasn't really our house on Seventh because in my dream it had a basement. My sister was there, and my dad, too, even though my dad had fucked off long before we were on Seventh, but anyway… At some point I went into the kitchen and there were cookies in the oven. I asked my mother what kind they were and she said, 'Spelling mistake cookies.' I forget the rest of the dream, but when I got up I remembered the spelling mistake cookies and thought it was a punchy phrase. Seems like it would make a good title. Anyway, it would pique people's curiosity."

"But it has nothing to do with our project."

"So what! We can always cobble a connection together after the fact. But we wouldn't even need to: unrelated titles are artistic. Think of Ray Bradbury's *I Sing the Body Electric*, or anything by Amélie Nothomb, or even *The Death of the Pterodactyl* by our friend Sébastien…"

"I don't find *Spelling Mistake Cookies* very artistic. It sounds more like a children's book for five- to eight-year-olds."

"So you're rejecting my suggestion?"

"Er…did you say you'd given the chapters titles?"

"Yes. So?"

"Well, if we had to, we could use it as a chapter title."

"Yeah, okay. But have you got anything better to suggest?"

"Not right now. But, you know, I don't think we'll come up with something just brainstorming cold. We both need to think about it and then compare ideas later. Better still, let's set up a "titles" file on the computer, and when we get an idea we'll add it to the list. When we've got a decent number, we'll sort through them. What do you think?"

I agreed it was sensible, so we did that. To kick things off, we both had to come up with a title, preferably bad, so that it would be easy to improve on it. I christened the file with *The Atheist Horsewoman* and Jude carried on with *The Evil Post-It Note*. Yes, it really could only get better. Dear reader, as you have in your hands the finished product, with a beautiful cover, a beautiful ISBN number, and gushing thanks to the Arts Council, you must already know the title we chose. Admit it, it's a pretty impressive title! I have no idea what it will be, but I know we'll find something spectacular, I have faith in us.

x···19···x

AN IMPOSSIBLE-TO-REFUSE OFFER

Sébastien was apparently convinced by my theory that the best way to get over his infatuation was to spend time with me. Not only had he brought his business back to us (take that, Auger!), but he had noticeably increased his sub consumption in order to spend more time in my company. The things love makes us do! Fortunately, his shyness prevented him (at least for now) from asking me out. He contented himself with hints so discreet I could ignore them. But the whole frontman thing gave us something to talk about. *So, how's the masterpiece coming along? Full speed ahead, buddy, better start thinking of something clever to say for when you're on the radio. And I hope you've got nice clothes, because you can't go to an award ceremony wearing your work things.* I hid my ambition behind a wall of jokes, pretended to take it offhandedly; his surprise would be all the greater the day I waved a letter under his nose saying, "Yes, yes, Mr Daoust, we'd like to publish you, no doubt about it. Your earlier works were interesting, granted, but this one is frankly genius. Contract to follow by next post."

He was, however, a little too involved in the project for my liking, gathering information about Bird-in-Hand, bursting with childish delight when he taught me some detail about the Amish's secret life. Obviously, I couldn't send him packing. And I have to admit he proved useful when it was time to fill in the grant application. He'd already been through it and he knew exactly what the people who sit on the selection committees wanted to hear, knew the buzzwords that turned on the literati, and knew how to create that fake depth that takes in even people who've seen it all before. I have to give him that: he knows how to write. If he'd bullshitted with as much panache in his books, he'd have permanently been in Renaud-Bray's recommended reads. (Because what is a good novelist, if not an ace bullshitter?) I didn't let myself reread part C ("Description of Writing Project") of our application, with its references to Goethe, Cormac McCarthy, and some unknowns, and fancy words like *intertextuality* and *paradigm*. The worst part was that he'd done it all off the cuff, without even a rough draft, at a Subway table. Of course, any resemblance between part C and the manuscript I'm in the process of writing is entirely coincidental, but who'd notice that? Do you really think there are civil servants at the Arts Council whose job it is to trawl through published novels to make sure they match the descriptions in their funding applications?

In short, everything was tootling along nicely until the day before we posted our application, when we read the conditions one last time to make sure our file wasn't missing anything. That's when we spotted a detail that had escaped us: there'd be a waiting period of four months after the deadline before we'd receive a response. Since we were still a month away from the deadline, that meant five months before the cheque landed in our mailbox—or rather, Sébastien's mailbox. That took us to early August. Shopping for a car, renewing our driver's licences (you had to take another test if it expired too long ago, we'd discovered), and preparing for it all would take, we reckoned, between two and three weeks. We'd therefore be lucky if we managed to set off before the first of September. We tried to look on the bright side (Pennsylvania must be very beautiful in autumn, and since it would be the off-season we could take advantage of better prices, and the restaurants would be less busy), but for people like us who aren't used to thinking about the future (what's the point? Our lives are as repetitive as wallpaper designs), September seemed incredibly far away. Virtually a figment of the imagination. But we didn't really have much choice.

With that in mind, Jude proposed revising the total of our grant application downwards. Since we had five months before we left, it would give us time, as long as we worked hard, to gather a good thousand dollars, maybe more. Moreover, by coming across as less greedy, we would increase our chances of a favourable response. In theory it wasn't a bad idea, but I pointed out that working hard had never been our strong suit. It was then that he pronounced this completely implausible sentence: "Yeah, but if I work too, it'll happen without us even noticing." It took me only a few seconds to convince him that this was a bad idea (Subway probably wasn't going to welcome me with open arms when we got back, and until I could find something else, his welfare cheque would be our only source of income), but his lips truly had formed that sentence, he really had conjugated the verb *to work* in the first-person singular! I tried to form a mental image of him going to meet managers and team leaders, a stack of CVs under his arm, shaking hands and proclaiming in an enthusiastic voice his desire to cook French fries or clean toilets, but my imagination couldn't make it that far. I had to admit, though, that the second part of his idea was sensible: by asking for a little less money, we'd be less likely to scare off the bureaucrats. So we did it: we brought out the Wite-Out, we read everything through one last time, and off we went to drop the letter in the mailbox.

The next day, at Subway, I told Sébastien how disappointed we were at the idea of being forced to hang around for five long months before weighing anchor. After listening to my lengthy grievances on the topic, he made the following suggestion: "You should buy the car and pass your test now. Then you'll be all set to take off when the cheque shows up."

"Um…if I could get my hands on four or five thousand dollars just like that, I wouldn't need to bleed the Arts Council."

"I can lend you the money. I'm not worried about you paying me back: don't forget the cheque will be made out to me. I'll just keep what you owe me and give you the rest."

"Do you have money?"

"A bit."

"From rowboats or royalties?"

"Neither. Definitely not royalties. When my mother died, I got her life insurance. I also sold her house."

"Your mother's dead?"

"Well, she's ashes in an urn… I don't think she's going to pull through."

"I never know what to say when—"

"Don't worry. Think about my offer instead. I can easily lend you a few thousand dollars without going into the red. Interest-free."

"I don't know what to say about that either."

"Accept. It would make me happy."

"There's just one detail you're forgetting."

"What?"

"On the Arts Council website they point out that there isn't enough dough for everyone who comes begging. In fact, they only say yes to around twenty per cent of the requests they get. I think our application is good, but there's no guarantee."

"True. Without the grant it would just take you longer to pay me back. But I'm in no rush. I have confidence in you, either way."

At the moment some customers came in, which got me out

of replying straightaway. The offer was tempting, and I suppose came at least partly from a good place. But only partly, because I couldn't help guessing his motive: if we didn't get the grant, I'd have to pay him back in instalments of $200 a month, which would link me to him for at least two years. In an ideal world I'd be his girlfriend, and we'd spend all our free time together, eating in restaurants, going to the theatre, doing projects, having sex, but he recognized that this scenario was unrealistic, so he was prepared to lower his sights, being content with my friendship, maybe having coffee together in town or watching a film in his living room, my head in his lap, and perhaps once in a while, after a well-lubricated dinner, I might let him do things to me, but he knew I wasn't on board with that plan either, so he really wanted to downgrade even further to a creditor–debtor relationship, if you could call it a relationship. Keeping me in his life one way or another. Wouldn't accepting his offer be abusing the situation? (From a strictly literary perspective, I must say this works out well: Mr Fisher points out that it's good for a character to experience a moral dilemma; it helps the reader identify with them. "Quickly confront your main character with a choice, put him or her in a state of conflict or crisis" [*Advice to a Young Novelist*, page 85].) For five minutes I served customers and weighed up the pros and cons. The idea of finding myself at his mercy (okay, maybe "at his mercy" is a bit melodramatic) for the next few years gave me no small amount of anxiety, but the loan would give us the chance to get going instead of twiddling our thumbs waiting for the Arts Council response, and that could be worth a bit of anxiety. In any case, if we didn't get the grant, we wouldn't be going to Bird-in-Hand, in which case we could sell the car and pay Sébastien back that way, at least partially. "Yes, okay."

"Okay?"

"I would like you to advance us the money for the car. If you're sure it's not a problem."

"I'm sure."

"Well, uh, thanks."

I ran all the way home, keen to tell Jude the news, but he wasn't in. He'd left me a note: "Gone to my mother's to do laundry. Hoping to get invited to stay for dinner. See you later." To kill time while I waited for him to come back, I thought I'd take a look at the classifieds websites for a vehicle, but I soon realized I didn't even know what to search for—make, model, body type, year, mileage, price, etc. What did we want, exactly? Would this 2003 four-door Mazda Protogé5 with 89,150 kilometres on it (AM/FM stereo, air conditioning, CD player, hubcaps, passenger airbag, fabric interior), sold by someone in Saint-Nicéphore, suit us? Who knows? It appeared to be fitted with a 1.8 litre engine. Is that good? I'd vaguely imagined rolling up at the dealership and announcing, "I'm looking for a good car between four and five thousand dollars."

"What colour, little lady?"

"Green, sir."

"Well, here's my best green car in your price range."

"It's perfect. Here's the money."

"Here are the keys."

But apparently it was going to be more complicated than that. We were probably going to have to ask Jude's father to negotiate for us, otherwise we were highly likely to get screwed over. So I decided to abandon the search for the moment and to have a shower while I waited for Jude. As I got undressed, my gaze fell on the copy of *13 Mechanical* on my dresser, and I was suddenly filled with a painful feeling toward its author, a mixture of guilt and pity, with perhaps a hint of inexplicable anger. Something unattractive. I said earlier I wasn't the biggest bitch around, but right then I had serious doubts about that. In a completely irrational way, I thought I might feel a little less wretched about Sébastien if I gave his book another chance. I opened *13 Mechanical* and started to read the first story in the collection, "Puppies for Sale." Maybe this time, if I made an effort, if I read carefully, if I focused on every nuance, I'd manage to see the text's beauty.

Puppies for Sale

Do you think I'll manage to sell my dachshunds before they get too old? Is this your first time here? Don't you think it's a funny name for a bar? Do you think it's easy to kill someone? Do you remember, in Heavenly Creatures, *the trouble Kate Winslet and her friend had beating the woman to death with the brick? You've never seen* Heavenly Creatures? *Aren't you taking your coat off? Does blood come out in the wash? Do you want to get a big pitcher? What should I do with five dachshunds in a one-bedroom apartment? Who are they playing tonight? What's the score? Why is the waitress giving them peanuts at the next table but not us? Are you sure you want to commit a murder tonight? Wouldn't we have been better off going with a blunt weapon? Will you be brave enough to stick a knife into a human being? Do you think Nana will get depressed when her puppies have left? Who just scored? Don't you think that big guy next to the jukebox looks mean? Who'd miss him if he was found dead in an alley tomorrow morning? Have I told you already that you are ridiculously beautiful? In your opinion, what's the rate of solved murders in real life? Have you noticed that it's always an earthling who wins Miss Universe? Do you think it's fixed? How about a vodka to warm our hearts? Do you think people will realize they aren't purebred?*

Oh, screw it! I just can't do it. It looks like I'm going to be the biggest bitch around, after all.

PART TWO

By Jude (with comments from Tess)

✖ ··· 20 ··· ✖

TESS'S INSTRUCTIONS
(Anything to Slack Off)

Okay, I've already told you this, but I'll write it down for you as a reminder. My last chapter was number 19, so start with 20. You can start again at 1 when you start a new section, obviously, but I think it's better to keep on with the momentum we've got going. Read over what I've written a couple of times and try to go on in the same sort of style so that rewriting isn't too tricky. By that, I don't mean just imitate me brainlessly and shut off your own creativity, but, for example, I've used "on" instead of "nous" for "we," which is border-line wrong and is giving me all sorts of grammatical issues, but in the end it came naturally, so carry on the same way, for better or worse. I've also decided, completely arbitrarily, to address a theo-retical reader, so when you talk to your audience, write "reader" or "dear reader" in the singular. Also, finish Mr. Fisher's two works as quickly as you can, if possible without getting mad at him when he cites the classics without having read them. I saw the page you'd turned down in Advice to a Young Novelist *and frankly we can't exactly say you're going at it at full steam. (Gogol will wait; he's dead and you've already read him ten times.) What else? Chapter titles in bold, two line spaces at the end of a chapter, one between the title and the chapter, italics for long quotes, etc. Anyway, if in doubt look back at my section or ask me for clarification. I know*

I've scared you a bit with how intensely I've been working on this, but it's because I need to set the scene, as they say in the business. But now that the scene is set and the narrative has reached the present moment, you'll only need to write on days when something important happens. Oh yes, and while I think of it: if it works out, write something about how we met the neighbour—I promised to do it but didn't have a chance. I suggest you start your section by introducing yourself using the same little questionnaire I did. The address is in the favourites. Good, now that's all done and dusted.

And there I have a very low-effort first chapter. [Yeah, now get on with some work!]

✖ ··· **21** ··· ✖

INTRODUCING JUDE

1. What time is it? *2:28.*
2. First name. *Jude.*
3. Age. *32.*
4. Height. *Six foot, according to my driver's licence, but in reality a little less.*
5. Eye colour. *Brown.*
6. Hair colour. *Brown.*
7. Star sign. *Capricorn.*
8. Hometown. *Grand-Mère.*
9. Brothers and sisters. *One brother.*
10. Have you ever been in love? *Yes, every two weeks. Currently in love with the girl in the white coat who plays with her dog in the yard at Laflèche College.* [That's because you haven't seen her up close: she's got a big nose.]
11. Do you think anyone has ever been in love with you? *I'd bet my life that the girl in the white coat is secretly in love with me.*
12. In your opinion, what do people think when

they see you for the first time? *I live in Grand-Mère: nobody ever sees me for the first time.*

13. Favourite film. Two Evil Eyes, *by Dario Argento and George Romero.*
14. Favourite book. A Raw Youth *by Dostoyevsky.*
15. Favourite song. *"Leave a Light on for me" by Belinda Carlisle.*
16. Favourite TV program. *Hockey Night in Canada.*
17. Best quality? *Flexibility.*
18. Biggest fault? *Crudeness.*
19. Do you believe in God? *No.*
20. What's your computer wallpaper? *A fat naked lady, put there by the neighbour. He finds that kind of thing funny.*
21. City or country? *Country.*
22. Winter or summer? *Winter.*
23. Where do you see yourself in ten years? *Here.*
24. What are your aims in life? *To spend two months in Pennsylvania.*
25. Name of your best friend. *Tess.* [That's better!]
26. Do you have a lucky charm? *The TV remote.*
27. If you could meet anyone you wanted, dead or living, who would it be? *Elizabeth Siddal.*
28. What's on your walls? *A sketch of Elizabeth Siddal, by I don't know who; Elizabeth Siddal as Ophelia in Millais's painting; Elizabeth Siddal playing the harp, with flowers in her hair, in a Rossetti painting.*

29. What's under your bed? *Boxes.*
30. Favourite meal? *Tess's mother's bouilla-baisse.*
31. Clothing style. *Salvation Army.*
32. Do you like your job? *Not applicable.*
33. Where would you like to be right now? *Bird-in-Hand.*
34. Do you think we are alone in the universe? *Who's "we"?*
35. Who's your hero? *Um . . .*
36. What word or expression do you overuse? *Good question, I'll have to ask Tess.*
37. What are you afraid of? *Tess dying.* [Even though I've told you I'm immortal.]
38. When was the last time you lied? *Yesterday, when I ticked "yes" to the question "Are you actively looking for work?" on my monthly declaration.*
39. Do you think you have a supernatural power? *I can communicate telepathically with the girl in the white coat who brings her dog to play in the yard at Laflèche College.*
40. Do you believe in soulmates? *Of course!*
41. Which historical figure would you like to be? *Dante Gabriel Rossetti. (If a pre-Raphaelite painter counts as a historical figure.)*
42. What would you get as a tattoo? *Nothing.*
43. What are your political views? *I read somewhere that Québec Solidaire was proposing an increase in social security payments. So Québec Solidaire.*
44. Who did you vote for in the last election?

I'm not registered to vote.

45. What is your biggest regret? *I don't do enough to have any chance of regretting anything.*

46. What's the first thing you do when you get up in the morning? *Pee.*

47. What's the last thing you do before going to bed? *Take out my contacts.*

48. At what age do you think you'll die? *I don't know. How about 130?*

49. Are you happy? *Why the fuck should I be?*

50. What time is it now? *3:45.*

✗ ··· 22 ··· ✗

IN WHICH WE LEARN THE EXTRAORDINARY WAY IN WHICH TESS AND JUDE MET THEIR IDIOTIC NEIGHBOUR

Okay, I know it shouldn't really go here, but there's nothing new to report right now and it doesn't fit any better anywhere else either, so I'm going to tell you, since I've been asked to, the story of how we met the moron who lives in the basement. It's a pretty amazing story, you'll see. [A plethora of narrative units coming up! Well done!]

At that time (we're talking around three years ago here), I spent a lot of my leisure time smashing up Krauts and Japs in *Call of Duty: World at War* on Xbox 360. Early every afternoon I'd make myself some tea, fire up the machine, choose my team (red army, naturally: I tried to fight for the Wehrmacht once but my heart wasn't in it, it was awful shooting the good Russians), and wait until there were enough participants to start playing. Although there were a lot of us on the network, I often saw the same names coming up because I logged on at the same time every day, and I flattered myself that I knew some of them pretty well. For example, Louvikov was a coward, the kind of guy who'd skulk in your shadow to make sure you'd be the one to take a bullet if you were ambushed; Scarface76, on the other hand, was a good team player, and would always leave you first-aid kits if he could see that you were more banged up than him; Badkid (who we suspected was a girl, for no particular reason: he/she didn't even have a microphone) was a crack sniper but had a tendency to ignore the leader's orders, etc. In *Call of Duty*, like all online multiplayer games, English is the working language, but you often end up finding out the nationality of your teammates, most of whom revert instinctively to their mother tongue in times of tragedy: "Putain! Fait chier!"; "Fuck!"; "Mrdat!"; "Schwanzlutscher!" (wow, we've got a German in the unit!) "Pukimak!"; "Horebukk!"; "Mierda!" I wasn't exempt from this rule, and occasionally I let slip, for example if I had the misfortune to step on a landmine, a heartfelt "Hostie de calice!" before I gave up the ghost; or let out a "Kin, mon tabarnak!" if I managed to bayonet a particularly tenacious enemy. One day, when I was lying in wait with TheMidnightRambler behind a ruined church in a dangerous sector in Stalingrad, I took a bullet in the thigh when I thought I was covered. "Ciboire!" I exclaimed. I heard my companion guffaw. "What's so funny?" I asked him, a bit peeved. "It's just funny to hear someone speaking Québécois," he replied. Well! I'd been on a team with this TheMidnightRambler for weeks without ever suspecting he was a compatriot. As the bullets whistled past our ears and mortar shells made rocks and clumps of earth rain down, we started up a conversation. "Where are you from exactly?" he asked me.

"Grand-Mère. It's about half an hour away from Trois-Rivières."

"Are you serious? I'm from Grand-Mère too."

"You're kidding me!"

"I'm really not!"

I couldn't see why he would have made it up, but it was too much of a coincidence for me to just take him at his word. Today 30 million Xbox 360s have been sold around the world (so let's say a few million less if we go back a couple of years), and *Call of Duty: World at War* was one of the most popular titles in 2008.

Around the world there were probably a few hundred thousand of us playing regularly. It was therefore highly unlikely, statistically speaking, that two guys living in the same godforsaken hole in Centre-Mauricie should find themselves next to each other under enemy fire, trying to stop General von Weichs's troops from crossing the Volga. "All right, prove it: what are the first three digits of your phone number?"

"Five three eight."

"And what's your closest store?"

"I'd say Videotron or Paquin Furniture."

"..."

"Hey! JudeTheObscure, you still there?"

"Um…yes. I'm just falling off my chair. You're not going to believe this, but I can see Paquin Furniture from my window."

"You're on Sixth?"

"Fifth. Corner of Fourth Street."

"Now I'm the one falling off my chair… Hang on, let's try something…"

"What?"

"Turn the TV volume down."

"Done."

"Right, now I'm going to bang on the ceiling three times. Well?"

"Fuck me, I can't believe it! You're that long-haired guy who listens to Slayer…"

"And you're the guy who lives with the girl with permanent bitchface…" [Huh! You never told me that bit!]

"Um…yes, that's right. Tess."

"I didn't know you could hear my music."

"It doesn't bother us."

I invited him to come up, and five minutes later he was slumped on our couch, in the spot that quickly became known as "the neighbour's spot," his family-sized bottle of Carling Black

Label between his legs. When Tess came home from work that evening, and I told her all about how I got to know the bum from downstairs, she was as blown away as I was. In fact, the almost supernatural nature of this meeting stopped us, for a long time, from seeing what a hassle it really was. It took a good two months before I dared admit to myself that, back on that gloomy afternoon, I'd have been better off letting the Battle of Stalingrad play out without me. At worst, Hitler would have won, but that would have been a lesser evil. We have no defence against the neighbour; we can't even pretend we aren't in: he can hear us walking around. When I finally confessed to Tess how distraught I was, hoping to get a few words of comfort from her (like, "Come on, you couldn't have known…"), she drove the knife in further by noting that the meeting defied the laws of probability to such an extent that if I'd bought a lottery ticket that day instead of playing Xbox, we'd be millionaires now. Woe!

PART THREE

By Tess

✖ ··· 23 ··· ✖

CHEVROLET MONTE CARLO

It tickles me whenever I think about it: since yesterday we've been the owners of a vehicle. More precisely, a yellow 2003 Chevrolet Monte Carlo. By the way, you'll have noticed that Jude has just passed the torch back to me after coming up with almost exactly two thousand words (which includes his ingenious copying and pasting of my instructions), which contravenes the principles of balance between parties advocated by every literary theorist from Aristotle to Marc Fisher, and now you'll think we're ridiculous. But we've decided it's better this way. Besides, we did some research and learned that in author pairs there's usually one who writes. It guarantees stylistic consistency. (Although it would astonish me if you could detect any major differences between my writing and Jude's, unless you're one of those nit-pickers who imagines differences between 7UP and Sprite, between Molson and O'Keefe, or between political parties.) And above all, the thing is, I enjoy writing. (Whereas it frightens Jude a bit, who's always afraid of getting it wrong.) If I was a real writer, with published books and articles about me in *Lettres Québécoises*, I wouldn't be so keen to say such things; I'd say that writing hurts, that it rips my guts out, that it's a painful but necessary act, that kind of nonsense. But I don't see why I should try to fool you in this situation. Anyway, since yesterday we've been owners of a yellow Chevrolet Monte Carlo, and right now the neighbour is giving it condescending looks and trying to convince us that we've been screwed over. But we know it's really because he's stung to the quick that we didn't ask him for his opinion even though he prides himself on knowing everything there is to know about cars. "Well, 's none of my business, but you ought to have gone with Japanese. *This* is just a bundle of trouble, this guzzles twice as much gas as a Civic, and the parts on this one are always crapping out. At least in the old models you had an eight, but now they've come down to six. It'll take you a good ten seconds to get from zero to sixty." I let him talk. He's barking up the wrong tree if he thinks he's going to upset me with his Mr. Know-it-all blather. I have no idea what he's on about with this stuff about six and eight, but I can't even imagine a situation in my life right now when I'd need to get to a hundred kilometres an hour in under ten seconds.

However, I must admit that the experts do agree with him. Among others, Amyot Bachand, from auto123.com, talks about the Monte Carlo in a rather lukewarm fashion, but, in my opinion, if your mother named you Amyot, you ought to refrain from public discourse. Without completely flaming the Monte Carlo, he just about gives it a passing grade and describes it as "a good comfortable touring car, blessed with good, reliable roadholding." As for its good points, the size of the trunk means you can easily fit in two golf bags, apparently a major plus for Amyot. But on the performance side, things go downhill a bit: "A good twenty extra horsepower would would be nice, if not a supercharged engine like the one in the Pontiac Grand Prix coupe." If you say so, Amyot, if you say so. But if you're as pressed for time as all that, surely you could just leave your house a bit earlier. Apart from that, the Monte Carlo seems to have a comfortable and functional interior, and behaves pretty well (for a car, behaving means roadholding and braking), despite the brake pedal being too high.

On the same site, one Éric Descarries provides a second opinion, which more or less matches his colleague's, and finishes up his report by listing the Monte Carlo's specifications. It's like contemporary poetry or a spy film: you have no idea what's going on, but from time to time it's beautiful. Here:

```
Engine: V6 3.4l
Optional engine: V6 3.8l
Horsepower/torque: 180 hp at 5200 rpm/205
    psi at 4000 rpm
Optional engine: 200 hp at 5200 rpm and 225
    psi at 4000 rpm
Transmission: automatic four-speed
Optional transmission: none
Front brakes: disk
Rear brakes: disk
Standard safety features: ABS, antiskid
Front suspension: independent
Rear suspension: independent
Wheelbase: 2.807m
Length: 5.026m
Width: 1.836m
Height: 1.403m
Weight: 1515kg; 1535 kg (SS)
0-100km/h: 9.6s
Top speed: 190km/h
Turning circle: 11.6m
Trunk capacity: 447l
Fuel tank: 64.3l
Fuel consumption: 12.6l/100km
Tires: 225/60R16
Optional tires: 225/60R16 performance (SS)
```

```
Average insurance premium: $950
Overall warranty: 3 years/60,000km
Engine warranty: 5 years/100,000km
Rust warranty: 3 years/60,000km
Bodywork warranty: 6 years/160,000km
Head-on collision: 5/5
Side-impact collision: 3/5
Quebec sales of model in last year: 582
Depreciation: 47%
```

There are people on this earth for whom this business of 11.6-metre turning circle means something, who might exclaim, "Wow, 11.6 metres! Now that's what I call a turning circle!" Jude's father is one of those people. When we asked him if he'd like to advise us on the purchase of our car, he immediately replied, "Perfect, tomorrow morning we'll go to Grenier's in Saint-Étienne." Two words made us frown: "morning" and "go." We let the first pass without comment; we knew it wouldn't be any use arguing. Jude's father is one of those people who think that things should be done in the morning or not at all. So we gave in to his "morning," but as for his "go," we allowed ourselves to point out that these days it would be useless—if not absurd—to go in person to a dealership. I mean, what would we even find at Grenier's in Saint-Étienne-des-Grès? A hundred machines at the very most, while 329,000 vehicles were listed just on autohebdo.net. But that didn't impress him. According to him, there was only one way to do this: man to man. You never know what you're going to get on the internet. And we didn't need three hundred thousand cars, we only needed one. End of discussion.

So we found ourselves—Jude, his father, and me—the next morning, in the J.-M. Grenier lot, on Chemin des Dalles, Saint-Étienne-des-Grés. A very enthusiastic gentlemen (probably J.-M. himself, Jean-Marc, Jean-Marie, or Jean-Michel) welcomed us as if he'd always dreamed of meeting us, and immediately started showing off his cars to us, starting with the most expensive. Since he was talking solely to Jude's dad, we could wander around the lot as we pleased. We read the cars' technical specs, trying to unravel the mystery, throwing out theories about what a drivetrain could be or a limited-slip differential, playing at making each other guess the prices. "How much do you think this one is?"

"Okay...I'll go with three thousand five hundred."

"Way off! Fourteen thousand, my girl."

"Oh. Right. But that red one over there is much more attractive and only costs five thousand."

"But the red one is a 1998 and this is a 2007."

The first time we went past the Monte Carlo, we didn't even bother looking at its specs. In our minds, a car like that would cost an arm and a leg. They could have told us a six-figure sum and we wouldn't have been surprised. It was only at the very end that Jude, out of curiosity, went over for a closer look. "That can't be right!"

"What can't be right?"

"Guess how much it costs."

"Sixty thousand?"

"Ten times less! Can you believe it?"

"Six thousand?"

"Five thousand eight hundred, to be precise."

"That's almost in our price range."

"Yes...only $2,000 over it."

"And we're not the kind of people to go crazy over a car."

"No, we're not like that at all."

"But you've got to admit it's a damn fine machine."

"That's for sure."

"But obviously we'd be pretty ashamed of ourselves if anybody caught us swooning over a car."

"Yes, we'd have trouble looking at ourselves in the mirror

for a couple of days. Remember how awful we felt that time we downloaded the Rihanna album."

"Yeah, that made us feel pretty soiled."

We were interrupted by Jude's father, who was keen to show us a grey Mazda Protogé5, tagged at $4,900, but that Jean-Marie, in a splurge of generosity, would let go for $4,500. We wouldn't find a better deal, the two gentlemen were adamant on that score, it didn't even have a hundred thousand kilometres on it, and it'd had its rust coating done every year. We glanced at it quickly, but from our point of view it looked like any old car you might see on the road or in a parking lot. We nodded our heads with a great deal of conviction and spouted some enthusiastic onomatopoeia, just to show Jean-Marie that we weren't ungrateful, that we recognized the enormous favour he was doing us with his $400 discount. We finished up by saying we'd come back to pick it up tomorrow, to give us time to get the money together, and we parted with a manly handshake. As we left, we asked Jude's father what he thought of the Monte Carlo, for no reason in particular. He stared at the object for a few seconds, then just shrugged his shoulders and sniffed disdainfully. Jude says he used to have the same reaction when confronted with Jude's report cards. It doesn't make the top ten of his favourite childhood memories.

When we got home, I called Sébastien to arrange to meet him the next day. He could have just written a cheque, but he really wanted to be there. We could hardly say no, and in any case we needed a lift to Saint-Étienne. He'd come by and pick us up shortly after lunch. All this time he'd been desperate to come to our house, and now he finally had his excuse. Underneath it was the perfectly legitimate desire to see the family set-up of the girl of his dreams, but above all he wanted to meet Jude, the guy included in the "we" with which I start most of my sentences.

I was in the shower when he showed up, so they had to introduce themselves. That was pretty straightforward: thirtysomething males have a whole stack of things in common. Jude was playing Left 4 Dead when Sébastien came in. Two minutes later, the latter had a controller in his hands and the two of them were taking out zombies like old brothers-in-arms. On the way to J-M. Grenier, I sat in the back seat and they spent the best part of the journey bellyaching about Scott Gomez's salary and the holes in Hal Gill's defence. It wasn't until the outskirts of Saint-Étienne that I interrupted to talk business. "So, Sébastien, how much are you willing to lend us?"

Sébastien: Dunno… How much is this car?

Me: Four thousand five hundred.

Sébastien: That's fine.

Me: But could you trust us with six thousand?

Sébastien: Um…ye-es, it's just that it'll take you longer to pay me back if the Arts Council shits on our plans.

Me: That's no problem.

Jude: I see where you're going. Are you trying to say—

Me: Do you really want to drive a Mazda Protogé5?

Jude: Um…I don't really have an opinion on the subject. I've only known about the existence of Mazda Protogés for twenty-four hours.

Sébastien: Mazdas are reliable.

Me: Reliable, reliable—do you really want that to be the first word that comes into people's heads when they think about you? Like, Sébastien Daoust, he's reliable.

Sébastien: To answer your question, yes. There's nothing wrong with being reliable if you're a person. But I'd say it's an essential quality in a car.

Me: Is a 2003 Chevrolet Monte Carlo reliable, in your opinion?

Sébastien: I don't know, but it's definitely a poser's car.

Jude: Are you sure, Tess?

Me: Aren't you?

Jude: I am, actually. But my father won't approve...

Me: What *does* your father approve of?

Jude: Yeah, not much.

Sébastien: If I'm getting this right, you want to buy a Monte Carlo?

Jude and me: Yes.

We didn't waste time on niceties: when you do something on a whim, you need to hurry before the buzz fades. If Jude's father was definitely going to think we were idiots, Jean-Marie, for his part, seemed to approve of our choice. People tend to think you're astute when you're spending $6,000 at their business. The formalities completed, Sébastien invited us to a restaurant to celebrate. We'd have preferred to be alone, but, once again, we couldn't decently race off the minute we'd got what we wanted from him. We arranged to meet at Buffalo Wings at the bottom of Shawinigan. I drove with exaggerated care, like people taking their baby home from hospital after it's born, driving ten kilometres an hour below the limit, putting the signal on ages before the highway exit, even going as far as obeying the yield signs. (I'm the only one who can drive right now, having been able to renew my licence quite easily since I'd only stopped paying to renew it two years ago.) We gobbled up our spicy wings and finally extricated ourselves from Sébastien. On the way back, we didn't say a word. I stared at the road while Jude got to know the dashboard. After parking in front of our building, we stayed sitting in the car for a good half-hour, lost in our own thoughts. It was Jude who broke the silence: "Apparently we own something worth six thousand bucks..."

"And we're six thousand bucks in the red."

"Yeah. Mazda Protogé5, whatever. As long as it gets us from A to B. We can still exchange it and get the difference back, even if we look stupid in front of Jean-Marie."

"Mazda Protogés are shit! Admit that this is a dream car!"

"But it's not really our style. Don't you like us a bit less?"

"Weirdly, I think I like us a bit better."

"So do I, but I'm not sure I should."

✕⋯**24**⋯✕

JOURNEY BY CHEVROLET MONTE CARLO TO SAINTE-ANNE-DE-LA-PÉRADE AND ENVIRONS, WITH SOME NOTES ON THE HISTORY, TRADITIONS, AND CUSTOMS OF SAID PLACES

People who know what they're talking about, the neighbour being number one, are unanimous in thinking that the Monte Carlo's major flaw is excessive petrol consumption, that she's a bit of a gas guzzler, but since it's our first car, we have nothing to compare it to, and I should point out that it was a week before we saw its little needle drop to E for the first time. To begin with, we scarcely dared touch it. We went on our little car trips in the evenings when I came home from work, but we stuck to our walking routes, sensibly remaining inside the city limits. We headed down to the English quarter by Fifth Avenue, came back up on Sixth, drove to the Domaine neighbourhood along Eighth Street, and returned by Fifteenth, with a few variations if we were feeling adventurous. The Grand-Mère bridge was making eyes at us, but crossing the Saint-Maurice seemed to us as freighted with consequences as crossing the Rubicon was for Julius.

It took ten days or so for us to dare going somewhere we couldn't get to on foot. It must have been one in the afternoon, we weren't doing anything much, I was reading and Jude was trying to beat Soda Popinski in Punch-Out!! when suddenly he turned off the Wii, turned to me, and told me to get dressed, we were going to Sainte-Geneviève-de-Batiscan. I didn't ask what had inspired this destination—I knew perfectly well that he didn't know himself—nor what we were going to do once we got there, I simply complied, and ten minutes later we were crossing the bridge. We drove past Saint-Georges-de-Champlain without even bothering to look at it and took the 153 toward Saint-Tite, making a little hook by Lake Lafontaine. We have a thing for Lake Lafontaine. It's ten bungalows around a pond (so insignificant that Google Maps doesn't even mention it), far from everything, totally devoid of charm, and yet people still choose to live there. Returning to Saint-Tite, we turned on the way into the village to take the 159 to Saint-Séverin and Saint-Stanislas. At Saint-Stan, we took the 352 toward Saint-Narcisse, where not much happens on the 360 days when it's not the Solidarity Festival. (You can always see its vaguely pretty church with two gothic-inspired bell towers, if you like that kind of thing; if not, you'll have nothing to do there, except get excited about mattress making, which is the town's main industry.)

Coming in sight of Sainte-Geneviève-de-Batiscan, the original destination of our trip, we decided we didn't want to stop. We drove slowly, windows open, SoftRock blasting out, it was fucking glorious. We crossed the Batiscan River to the sound of "Dust in the Wind" and ran into the Saint Lawrence around Saint-Pierre-les-Becquets. There we took the 138 north and drove along the river to Sainte-Anne-de-la-Pérade. We thought briefly about pushing on to Grondines, but we were starting to get a bit peckish and, anyway, for our first real car trip we didn't want to leave the region. In Sainte-Anne-de-la-Pérade we also found a neo-gothic church with two bell towers, even more beautiful than the one at Saint-Narcisse, and a tommy-cod interpretive centre right at the entrance to the village, which we felt duty-bound to visit. The lady at the ticket desk told us they were closing in half an hour, but a swift glance around the exhibition room told us that it ought to be enough time to see everything. For eight dollars a head, we could watch a couple of tommy cod in an aquarium, look at a diorama of the village of huts on the river, as well as several displays explaining the habits of the tommy cod and the history of ice fishing. (Tommy cod used to spawn in the Saint-Maurice, but when industrialization rendered that waterway too polluted, they moved down to the Sainte-Anne River. In 1938 one Eugène Mailhot, who'd come to cut blocks of ice for the family icebox, noticed them there and built the first cabin by the river. Who'da thunk it! After we'd reeled off every single joke we could think of about how it must have been one tasty fish for us to fork out eight bucks, we set off to look for somewhere to eat. We followed Lanaudière Boulevard, which seemed to be the main street, and after driving for ten minutes we came across the Motel Café la Pérade. It didn't look like much but it was there or nowhere… We ordered two pints of the least terrible beer, which we downed in three gulps before ordering two more. The alcohol had more of an effect than usual; after ten minutes we were already starting to stumble over our words and snigger stupidly at nothing. Our excitement must have contributed significantly to our light-headedness. We couldn't get over the fact that here we were having a drink in an establishment of whose very existence we'd been unaware when we got up that morning. We'd barely driven a hundred kilometres, yet we were almost stunned that the people spoke our language and accepted our money. In any case, we thought ourselves very daring.

Although we hadn't had anything to eat since lunch, we weren't particularly hungry. We were fine just eating some almonds from the vending machine and a bit of cheese from the Pichet Dairy, situated right next to the Motel Café la Pérade. After my third pint, I declared that I was going to stop there; after all, I was the one driving. "But there aren't any police in Sainte-Anne-de-la-Pérade," Jude pointed out. "If we head back through the villages, there won't be any risk. They're all under the jurisdiction of the Quebec police, and they only have two cars to cover an area the size of Normandy. If you ever wanted to kill someone in Saint-Roch-de-Mékinac, you'd just need to report a robbery in Notre-Dame-de-Montauban and the coast would be clear for a good hour." After I'd decided that what was coming out of his mouth was simple good sense, I ordered one last one for the road. After that, we got back in the Monte Carlo and tried to do our journey in reverse, the only difference being that we went through Saint-Prosper rather than Saint-Narcisse, which would be a perfect example of the expression "six of one, half a dozen of the other." At that time of day, the show *P.S. Tenderness* was playing on SoftRock: people (mostly women) phoned in to dedicate a song to a loved one. ("I'd like to dedicate 'Unchained Melody' to my little Coco, who's working all night. From your Gisèle, who loves you and can't wait to hug you"; "It's already been two weeks since you left, Lucette, my heart is broken, I would dearly love to erase the past so that everything can go back to how it was before. Just for you, here's the song that was playing when we met: 'How Can I Tell You,' by Marie-Chantale Toupin," etc. It was almost unbearable at times.) We went through Saint-Prosper, Saint-Stan, Saint-Séverin, Saint-Tite, and Hérouxville belting out Pierre Bachelet, Didier Barbelivien, and Julien Clerc at full volume, and before we knew it we were heading back over the bridge. We went slowly down Sixth, mildly astonished that everything was exactly as it was when we'd left. The neighbour was pottering about on his balcony. We could see just by looking at him that he'd have given ten years of his life to know what we'd been up to all this time, but he had enough self-control to ask us no questions whatsoever, so we just exchanged polite small talk as we passed. I was so drunk on alcohol and good humour that I even spoke to him myself.

It was only ten o'clock when we got into the apartment, but we were out like a light and slept until the next morning. Strong emotions suck out all your energy, even if you don't notice it at the time.

✗···**25**···✗

A LITTLE MORE GEOGRAPHY?

As everyone knows, the first step is what really matters. After this journey to the realm of the tommy cod, our boldness knew no limits. As soon as we had the cash to fill the tank (around fifty dollars, depending on fluctuations in gas prices), we went onto Google Maps to choose a destination and plan an itinerary, threw a few things into a cooler, stopped off to buy a case of beer, and set off. For example, we might decide to go and see what was up in Saint-Côme. So we'd leave Shawinigan, wisely waiting until we'd left civilization behind (that is, getting as far as Saint-Boniface) to pop the cap off our first beer. After Saint-Alexis-des-Monts and Sainte-Angèle-de-Prémont, we left 819 country and entered unknown territory. Shivers of excitement! Often, when we arrived in a village, we parked the car and went for a little walk, so we could stretch our legs, piss out our beer, and see how they lived in Sainte-Émélie-de-l'Énergie or Saint-Damien (although we never found anything out about Saint-Damien, since we didn't see a single soul in the streets of that municipality, which is, let me just point out in passing, one of the biggest in Quebec, with its 417 square kilometres. It's a long way from the Gaspé's 1,447, but it's still nearly as much as the entire island of Montreal.

Once we arrived at our intended destination, we'd take a

break to eat the food we'd brought, or, budget permitting, we graced some local establishment with our custom. In Saint-Côme, for example, we ate at the Rhythm of Time Inn, which cost us an arm and a leg, but I'd just got my tax return back so we really needed to celebrate that. After doing some sightseeing for an hour, the time it took for the wine to wear off, we came back by Saint-Alphonse-Rodriguez, Sainte-Marcelline-de-Kildare (which truly does exist, I promise), Saint-Ambroise-de-Kildare, Joliette, and Lavaltrie, where we picked up the 40 and then the 55 to get us home.

Our next journey took us to the heartlands of the Chaudière-Appalaches, to Irlande, Saint-Adrien-d'Irlande, Saint-Ferdinand, and Sainte-Sophie-d'Halifax, which, as the name does not suggest, is situated slightly south of Plessisville. We also went to Kiamika, in the Hautes-Laurentides (to orient you, it's very close to Val-Barrette and a tiny bit east of Saint-Aimé-du-Lac-des-Îles), and La Tuque, that other ridiculously large municipality (big enough to fit New Hampshire inside it), where we attended a hotly disputed wet T-shirt competition at the Chez Bo bar and where we stayed overnight for the first time, at the Ideal Motel, in case you're wondering (fifty dollars for a double room).

Even though we'd become veritable Jack Kerouacs, we carried on with our virtual travelling. Now that we knew how brave we could be, we wondered if we hadn't been too timid in limiting ourselves to a thousand-kilometre radius. Pennsylvania was essentially our next-door neighbour, after all. Why not push on to Florida, to Two Egg, for example, west of Tallahassee? A trek of 2,600 kilometres. No, not Florida, we couldn't stand the climate. (We start grumbling when the mercury goes above twenty-five.) Arizona seems much more bearable, so we could set off for Allah, located 4,400 kilometres distant, and which shares with our own Lake Lafontaine the distinction of being ignored by Google Maps; or maybe for Aztec Lodge, northeast of Phoenix, right in the heart of Usery Mountain Regional Park. From there, we could take the 88 toward Tortilla Flat and try to discover how many of the place's six inhabitants have read Steinbeck's *Tortilla Flat*. Then, come slowly back to Utah on the 87, going through Tonto Basin, Gisela, Star Valley, Strawberry, Lake Montezuma, Pilgrim Playground, and Pumpkin Center. (See Pumpkin Center and die!)

We might also decide to take a themed trip. For example, we could head down into Pennsylvania to King of Prussia, location of the second-biggest mall in the United States. (We're talking here about 260 square kilometres of shopping area, which is a bit larger than the surface area of Luxembourg.) Since it's probably impossible to see it all in a day, or even two, we could really go to town and make a reservation at the Dolce Valley Forge Hotel for a week, which offers, for the modest sum of ninety-nine dollars a night, the following services and amenities: restaurant, bar, twenty-four-hour reception, newspapers, non-smoking rooms, equipment for people with reduced mobility, elevator, safe, heating, shuttle service to the shopping centre, gym, outdoor pool, etc. On leaving King of Prussia, we'd head northwest, go around the Great Lakes, and stop in Bloomington, Minnesota, site of *the* biggest shopping centre in the United States, the famous Mall of America, with its 390 square kilometres (Norway), shared among more than five hundred shops (soon to be nine hundred). Then we'd make for the Ramada Mall of America, situated right next to this monster. Since the King of Prussia Mall would be fresh in our minds, we could compare them, like, "Yes, it's true that it's bigger than King of Prussia, but it doesn't seem quite as good." "There are more shops, true, but the eating was better in Pennsylvania," "Yeah, we're a million miles away from Trois Rivières's Galeries du Cap," etc. And then, having ventured so far west, we could just nip across North Dakota and Montana to come back into this country through Alberta and finish our tour with a trip to the West Edmonton Mall—the biggest shopping centre in North America, this one (and fifth in the world), with 570 square kilometres of floor space (not quite Kenya, but pretty close). After this last shopping orgy, we'd get on the Trans-Canada and zip back home, with stories to tell for the rest of our days. Obviously, the budget is the stumbling block in this whole enterprise. (What exquisite torture it would be to wander around West Edmonton Mall without a cent in your pocket!)

A less expensive idea would be to do the Lick Tour. Start at Lick, Ohio, then cross Cincinnati from north to south and stay a few days in Bone Lick State Park. Then off to Kentucky, fill up at Salt Lick, and retrace our steps to burn a few dollars at French Lick Resort Casino, situated in the charming village of French Lick, whose main claim to fame is being the birthplace of the legendary Larry Bird, one of the best players in NBA history, whose nickname was "the Hick from French Lick." After striking it rich at roulette and spending a few moments paying our respects at Mr. Bird's grave (if he's dead) or having our photograph taken with him (if he's alive), we'd race off to leap the 500 kilometres separating French Lick and Knob Lick, a hole so unimportant that not only does Google Maps snub it but nobody has even published an article about it on Wikipedia (where it is nonetheless possible to find information on the following subjects: "The problem of sexuality between men and mermaids in literature," "Benzedrine in popular culture," "List of fictional characters with nine fingers," "List of English words containing a q that is not followed by a u," "Cotard's Syndrome" [in which sufferers imagine they don't even exist], "Names of chemicals containing unusual words" [such as angelic acid and cadaverine], "Mucophagy" [or eating mucus], "Rapunzel syndrome" [sufferers of which eat their own hair], "The story of Mary Toft, a woman who claimed to have given birth to rabbits," "Historical figures who wore pointy hats," "Urban legends about the McDonald's chain,"

Adolf Hitler's vegetarianism," "chicken sexers" [people trained to determine the sex of poultry], "Nils Olav, the penguin colonel in chief of the Norwegian royal guard," "List of pigs in history," "Axinomancy" [or how to see the future with axes], "Religion in the Antarctic," "List of unrealized religious prophecies," "List of fictional chameleons," etc.). We'd stop briefly at Knob Lick before setting off again to meander across Kentucky, since most of the Licks are in that state: Lick Fork, Grants Lick, Lick Creek, Mud Lick, Spring Lick, Flat Lick, Paint Lick, Blue Licks (the site, in 1782, of the famous Battle of Blue Licks, in which Daniel Boone took part, and which was one of the last clashes in the War of Independence), Beaver Lick, Big Beaver Lick, Plumb Lick, May Lick, and Lickburg. After having exhausted all possible pleasure in Lickburg, we'd leave Kentucky at last and pop over for a quick look at some other nearby Licks: Lizard Lick, Black Lick, Lick Skillet, finishing up with Otter Lick, North Carolina. Then back on Interstate 95, lamenting for once that we have no social life and therefore nobody to whom we can brag that we've just done the Lick Tour.

Or why not a food theme? Starting in Cheesecake, New Jersey, and zigzagging southward, stopping off in Ham Lake, Sandwich, Hot Coffee, Oniontown, Sugar City, Bacon, Oatmeal, Picnic, Chocolate Bayou, Goodfood, and ending up, of course, in Florida, at Two Egg, where we'd get drunk in some neighbourhood bar while we worked up the courage to point out that "Egg" was missing an "s."

But we knew, even as we talked, that it was all just hot air, that we'd never set foot in Lizard Lick or Aztec Lodge. As ridiculous as it might seem to you, we'd come to believe that our business rightfully belonged to the Smucker family. We'd feel as though we were betraying them if we blew them off to go and hang out with rednecks in Tortilla Flat. In any case, we might well spend a chunk of cash going to Saint-Côme or doing cultural activities in La Tuque, but I bet once we reached Lancaster County we'd think we'd put enough tarmac between us and the Grand-Mère rock.

✗···**26**···✗

STEVE

Coming out of Gambrinus, we decided to walk back to the car via Des Forges, just to change things up. That's how we came to walk by Gosselin Photo's window display, where the same idea came to us both at the same time: you can't go on holiday without a camera.

You're probably going to ask what we were up to in Des Forges; you'll be thinking that you've completely lost track of what's going on, but don't worry, it's all deliberate: from the next paragraph, I'm going to be doing what's known as a flashback. I'll pick up where we were and I'll tell you everything that happened leading up to our trip to Gosselin Photo. There's nothing magical about it, it's a standard literary technique, it avoids the monotony of a strictly linear narrative and gives the reader the illusion that the text has a structure, that it is constructed. Mr. Fisher recommends that beginning authors do not try this route, but with nearly 120 pages under my belt I can hardly still be considered a beginner.

For weeks, nothing much happened. As soon as we had a few dollars to spend, we converted them into gas and set off on a trip. For example, if, after emptying our pockets, raiding the piggybank, and taking back our returnable bottles, we gathered together $17.46, we headed to Olco, looked the gas-station guy in the eye, and, without batting an eyelid, said to him, "Put in $17.46 of regular, please." Then we'd have a little discussion about how far we could get with that amount of petrol. "With eighteen bucks' worth of gas, I reckon we could make it to Lac-aux-Sables and back."

"I think that's a bit conservative, man. I reckon we could get as far as Rivière-à-Pierre, no trouble."

"Maybe at a push, but it'd be no bad thing to save a bit of petrol for our day-to-day errands."

"That's true. Lac-aux-Sables it is."

We knew we really should have been putting money aside. After paying for the car, which had cost us $2,000 more than we planned, we had exactly six thousand left to finance our trip. The obvious solution was to shorten our stay, but we refused to go that route. Instead, we decided to revise our estimates downward. I said above that a room for two at the Bird-in-Hand Family Inn would cost $127.65. However, a single room would only come to $98.79, a saving of almost thirty dollars a day. Jude has trouble sleeping in the same bed as me because apparently I fidget a lot in my sleep, but he'll have to manage for a few weeks. And when I said it would cost us $250 a day (including accommodation) to live, I was counting eating out three times a day, but I realize I was inflating things somewhat. Some mornings we can easily have a loaf of bread and a cup of coffee for breakfast, and buy something at the grocery store for lunch. Or just gobble a sandwich and a Mars bar from a vending machine. Basically, if we agree to not be too precious about it, we can easily get by with a $150 a day.

In fact, the only thing worrying us about the trip is this: what are we going to do with Steve? But before diving into this question, I really ought to introduce you to Steve.

When we met him, he was walking along the edge of the 155, at the Grandes-Piles exit, towards Saint-Roch-de-Mékinac.

To this day, we still don't know if he was actually planning to head all the way to Saint-Roch-de-Mékinac, but that would have been a ludicrous ambition: the fact that he could walk at all was pretty astounding. He was staggering all over the road so much that we had to slow down and veer over the yellow line to avoid him. Someone driving any faster might not have spotted him in time. "Hey, what's that?"

"I would have said a hyena, but I don't think there are any hyenas around here. A coyote maybe?"

"No, it was white with spots. I think it was just a rather unattractive dog."

"Perhaps we should help it…"

We parked the Monte Carlo in the Auto HiFi car park and walked back toward the animal. We told ourselves it was a lost cause, that he'd run off into the woods when he saw us, but maybe he'd let us get close and, if he was wearing a tag, we could phone his house so he could get home. He didn't flee when he saw us, he simply continued his laborious trotting toward Saint-Roch-de-Mékinac without glancing at us. He wasn't trying to snub us; I think it was more that his instincts were telling him that the next time he stopped might be the last. He had enough energy to keep moving, but he knew he'd never manage to overcome inertia again. What Jude had said was right: he was in fact a rather unattractive dog. In general shape he resembled a hare, but his genetic background must have included DNA from all possible canine species, except perhaps the Saint Bernard. His head was a bit like a collie's, but with the halfwitted eyes of a chihuahua and a muzzle like that of my cousin Karine's dog, a hideous Chinese crested called Marius. His ribs jutted out under his coat, a greyish-white speckled with black and brown spots. He was so thin that it was a bit of a stretch to talk of him as a three-dimensional being. We waited until he reached us and then fell into step behind him. I asked him all the usual questions in my most reassuring voice: "Who does this good little doggy belong to? What's doggy's name? Where's his house?" The answers to the questions were obvious ("Nobody," "I haven't got a name," "What's a house?"), but Caesar (the guy from *The Dog Whisperer*) claims that dogs can understand voice inflections. I wouldn't swear that I'd managed to earn his trust, but when we got back to Auto HiFi and I invited him to jump into the car, he only hesitated for a few seconds (the time it took to say to himself, "What have I got to lose?") before dragging himself, in all his pain and misery, onto the back seat.

We did a U-turn and went to the grocery store on Boulevard Ducharme in Grandes-Piles to buy some dog food. We picked up two cans of Dr. Ballard's (not the real one, the Compliments sort, I don't think Dr. Ballard's exists anymore), which the woman at the till was kind enough to open for us, and a *Journal de Montréal* to use as a plate. We served it to him that way, unceremoniously, in the car park. He started stuffing his face, looking worriedly all around, unsettled by the idea that nobody was coming to fight him for his feast. Once the last bite had been swallowed, he waited a few hopeful seconds for a second serving and then, seeing that none was forthcoming, got back in the car. We could see he was still hungry, but since it's not a good idea to overfill the stomach after fasting we ignored his imploring looks and set off.

We'd been driving in silence for five minutes when Jude asked, "So, what are we doing?"

"I don't know."

"We should give him a ride to the SPCA in Trois-Rivières. I think that's the nearest branch."

"If we take him to the SPCA they'll put him in a cage, and two weeks later they'll gas him. If that's our plan, we might as well just have left him to croak at the side of the road."

"Someone might adopt him."

"Have you actually looked at him? He's a nightmare on four

legs. Nobody's going to adopt him."

"So what should we do then?"

"Well…"

"You want to keep him?"

"Um…"

"We're not allowed to have pets, it's in our lease."

"It's in every lease, but I don't think Mrs. Rheault would grumble about it. She'll never even know anyway."

"You're right, but…"

"But?"

"A dog is a responsibility. It's a living thing that will rely on us for its survival and well-being. Doesn't that worry you?"

"Fucksake! We need every penny to keep ourselves alive. But what choice do we have? If we'd gone with our first idea of driving through Saint-Jean-des-Piles, we'd never have come across him and he'd probably have died before sunset."

"Yeah, why did we have to go farting around in Saint-Jacques-des-Piles?"

"We need to give him a name."

"We do indeed. Any ideas?"

"Hmm… No, but it should be something pretty wretched, pitiful, to match his appearance. Definitely not the name of an emperor or some mythological figure."

"What do you think of Steve? That's like the most loser name in the world. Go on, try and name one Steve who's succeeded in life."

"Steve McQueen, Steve Jobs, Steve Yzerman…"

"They're anglophones. But you must admit that in Quebec there's nothing more uncool than a Steve. It's usually people on welfare who give their children American names."

"Yeah, that's true. And he really does look like a Steve."

"Shall we go with Steve then?"

"Let's go with Steve!"

x ··· 27 ··· x

JUSTINE HAS A HUGE ASS
(Because I Keep My Promises)

Even with the windows open, the air in the car quickly became unbearable. It smelled kind of like that greenish juice that oozes out of dumpsters. There was no question of him setting foot in our place before just a teensy bit of freshening up. We stopped at my mother's house. While Jude herded Steve into the yard, I went to the bathroom to get shampoo, a towel, and an exfoliating mitt. André, my mum's husband, rushed over to find out what I was up to. "We're washing our dog." Torn between the distress our intrusion was causing him and his desire to seem cool, he simply pointed out that "Sylvie won't be superhappy when she sees you've used her exfoliating mitt and clean towel on a dog." I conceded the point and went out to rejoin Jude and Steve.

Steve didn't seem to particularly enjoy the stream of cold water, but he didn't run off; he waited stoically until it was over, gazing at us with his big, sad eyes, as if to say, "I was starting to believe that you might be good people, and now you're doing this to me. But fine, it's just so much like everything else that I can't even say I'm disappointed," or maybe that's just me over-analyzing. I gave him a good shampoo, rubbed him down with the exfoliating mitt, sponged him properly, and then went to throw away all the stuff we'd used during his bath while he tried to dry off in the sun.

Before we went home, we stopped by the veterinary clinic on the corner of Sixth and Eighth to pick up a big bag of Orijen brand dog food, two bowls, a collar, a leash, a hide bone, and a big cushion. Total: $72.85. We didn't say anything, but we were thinking, "The amount he's just cost us, this fucker'd better survive at least six months so we feel like we got our money's worth." Seeing our purchases, the lady at the checkout brilliantly deduced that we had just acquired a dog, and started talking to us about vaccinations, health records, and sterilization. We took her leaflet to shut her up and threw it into the next garbage bin we passed. We don't even have health records ourselves, so…

We put his food and cushion in the part of the living room where the computer is and pottered around for a bit while he got used to his surroundings. After one minute, he'd drunk all his water and gobbled up his Orijen ration. Apparently, you shouldn't drink when you eat, it's bad for your digestion, the water makes the food swell. I should think it's even worse if you've stuffed yourself with two cans of Dr. Ballard's an hour earlier. But nutritional advice is all very well for people who are used to eating every day. From Steve's perspective, this day was an anomaly. Such an abundance couldn't possibly last. In this situation, his basic survival instinct told him to make the most of it while it was there. Once his two bowls were empty, he looked over at his cushion, then, having judged it to be inedible, he lost interest in it and dragged himself up onto the couch, where he curled up into a ball and fell asleep immediately. He's still asleep as I write this, and he looks as though he's dreaming about running or digging a hole because he's twitching his feet and letting out little sighs.

"Twenty dollars for a cushion! He could have tried it, at least."

"Pah. We'll tell him that when he wakes up. For now, we've

got a bigger problem to solve."

"Such as?"

"Such as what are we going to do with him when we go to Bird-in-Hand? Have you thought about that?"

"Vaguely, but we aren't leaving right away. Anyway, we always solve our problems at the last minute."

"Yes, except that our problems usually revolve around us. If we behave like idiots, we're the ones who suffer. Now it involves Steve, and it's one of our responsibilities as his masters to make the right decisions about his well-being."

"But it's not really a problem: we'll just take him with us. It's easy to travel with a dog in the States—there are lots of pet-friendly hotels and even restaurants. Americans love their pets."

"But crossing the border with an animal is pretty tricky. They have to be registered and vaccinated, and you need all sorts of permits. Miles of forms to fill in and you come out of it a thousand bucks poorer. I know all about it: my grandmother's sister goes to Florida every winter and takes Muguet with her."

"So what should we do then?"

"We'll have to have someone look after him, but I can't think who."

"We could leave him here and ask the neighbour to come and feed him and take him out for a walk every day. He's always round here anyway, he might as well make himself useful once in a while."

"Are you crazy?! I wouldn't want to be in debt to the neighbour if my life depended on it."

"Who, then? My parents wouldn't want to because he'd probably fight with their cats, and your mother's afraid of dogs. Your sister, on the other hand..."

"She'll say she hasn't got time. That's her greatest pleasure in life, saying she hasn't got time."

"But she has got time. She lives close by, and she goes out

every day anyway to take Bilbo for a walk. She'd just need to pick Steve up on her way past. She could even keep him at her house, then he'd be company for Bilbo."

"Yeah, but she's still going to say she hasn't got time."

"Ask her anyway, we've got nothing to lose."

"As a last resort."

"This is the last resort. With your parents and the neighbour, we've pretty much been through all our acquaintances. Unless you ask Sébastien…"

"Then I really would feel as though I was taking advantage of his good nature."

"Can you think of anyone else?"

"Fine, give me the phone, I'll call my sister."

She picked up after four or five rings, like she does every time, to make it look as though she's busy. I revealed the reason for my call without beating about the bush. "Would you look after our dog for a month and a half this autumn while we're in Pennsylvania?"

"You've got a dog?"

"I wouldn't ask you to look after it otherwise. Actually, he's very new, we've only had him for an hour."

"Where did you buy him?"

"We found him."

"Oh. What kind of dog is it?"

"No particular kind. But you haven't answered my question."

"Yes, I'd love to."

"Really? It wouldn't be a bother?"

"Not a bit. Especially since you won't go."

"Why do you say that?"

"Because it's true. You won't go on a trip to Pennsylvania or anywhere else, and you won't do anything else either. How could I say such a thing? Jude or you on your own would be a millstone for anyone, but together you're like two millstones joined together, get it? I'm not saying that to be mean, and I've got nothing against Jude, but at some point you have to realize that—"

"Yeah, fine, you've already told me your millstone story, I know all that, but if I've understood you right, you're agreeing to help us because you're sure you'll never have to do it?"

"Something like that."

"Well, I'll accept your yes. We're what today—July 24? The money should arrive in about a month. Two weeks after that, we'll split and leave you the dog on our way past. I'll take you at your word."

"What money?"

"The money from the Arts Council for the book we're writing. I've told you about it, but you must not have been listening."

"You won't write any book."

"Want to bet?"

"If you want."

"If you're sure that we won't write a book, will you agree to let us call it *Justine Has a Huge Ass* or *Justine Has Stinky Feet*?"

"Sure. I can't wait for my signed copy of *Justine Has a Huge Ass*!"

"Well…I think we'd be happy to just call one chapter that. But we're going to do it, and you're going to get your signed copy."

"Cool."

"I'll call you a couple of days before I bring Steve round."

"Steve?"

"The dog."

"Right. Perfect."

✗···**28**···✗

THE DAY OF BIG SURPRISES

Steve quickly adapted to his new life as a pet dog. The idea of being taken care of, of seeing food fall from the sky at regular intervals, hasn't damaged his self-esteem in the slightest. He's accepted it as his due. A real welfare bum at heart. He even staged a mini-hunger strike one day when we gave him chicken-and-vegetable Orijen instead of beef. (But we stood firm and he cracked after fifteen minutes.) He looks a little less bony now that he's put on a bit of weight, but, let's be honest, he's never going to win any beauty competitions. On the other hand, he's as clever as a little monkey. He goes to find his leash when I say it's time to go out; when I put a treat on his nose, he waits for my signal before snapping it up; he's learning to play dead, but he's not there yet. If we lived in a big city, we could get up a routine and put on a show in tourist areas. We'd get rich. Even though I'm the one who teaches him all his tricks, even though I'm the one who spoils him the most (I always let him finish my plate and I give him the remains of my drumsticks), I must confess he has a marked preference for Jude. He loves me a lot, for sure, but if there was a fire and he could save only one of us, I'm under no illusions. Jude is truly the Eighth Wonder of the World. All he has to do is open his mouth and Steve starts thumping his tail on the floor.

Once, a couple of years back, Jude's mother took in a little stray cat who, once settled, refused to ever set foot outside again. (Tempest, her name was, and she too would never have won a ribbon at any cat show.) She seemed to be afraid the door would shut for good behind her if by some misfortune she ever crossed the threshold. Her former owners must have kicked her out, so we could never get her to risk it again. To begin with, I was afraid of things going the same way with Steve, that his weeks (months?) of living wild might have put him off the outdoors and that he might become a couch potato. But no, he loves going out; if it was up to him, he'd spend eight hours a day outside. His favourite walk is the following: we take Third as far as Grand-Mère Shoes (yes, I know it's not been Grand-Mère Shoes for ages, but we oldies stay attached to the old names: the shop across from Matteau's place is still Claire Corsetry to me; The Source is still Bonbon Thérèse, etc., and it will be that way until I die); anyway, we get as far as Grand-Mère Shoes and then head into the woods by the hill that goes up to the Maurice XM snowmobile club. There, a network of paths takes us to the other side of the hill, onto Eighteenth Avenue (you might think there wouldn't be two streets with the same name in a single municipality, but there are indeed two Eighteenth Avenues in Grand-Mère, this one and the one in the Domaine. We turn onto Chemin des Cormiers, walk along Beau-Rivage, and come back by Chemin des Marronniers. We rejoin civilization, so to speak, by Eighth Avenue South, the official name of the Grand-Nord hill. We could do this loop in three hours, but we always spend ages in the forest, where Steve likes to chase animals both real and imaginary.

Usually we go for a second walk after dinner, but not such a long one. We make do with going to Rivière Park, for example, where I sit on a bench while Steve enjoys sniffing other dogs' behinds, or yapping at the ducks from the bank. Most of the time,

Jude skips his turn for the evening walk. So I was alone with the dog last Monday evening when Seb came up to me. "I called your place. Jude said I'd probably find you here," he said, sitting down next to me. His turning up like this worried me slightly. It was so not his way to impose. We'd seen each other a few times in recent months, to have coffee or just to stroll along Sixth, and each time he'd gone to the trouble of phoning in advance. "Uh, Tess…it's Sébastien… Um…I was just wondering if you'd like to have coffee with me this afternoon. I mean, only if you want to, if you've got nothing else on. But…um…no big deal." So his turning up like that, without warning and without seeming bothered by his daring, made me suspect that he had something important to tell me, but, since I'm not optimistic by nature, I didn't imagine for a single second that it might be good news. Instead, I was imagining catastrophic scenarios, like him falling to his knees and presenting me with a jewellery box while giving me a speech about uniting our destinies. "Jude told me you'd gone out to walk the dog. I guessed from that that you had a dog."

"Very good, Holmes."

"Which one is it?"

"The white one with spots over there."

"It doesn't look like a dog."

"You get used to it."

"It's a total skeleton! Don't you feed it?"

"You'll never believe it, but he's tripled in size since we've had him."

"Incredible! What's his name?"

"Steve."

"It suits him."

"…"

"Apart from that…um…how's the book coming along?"

"Not bad. If we get back from the States in November as planned, I should manage to finish over the winter, edit in the spring, and send it off in time for the autumn season."

"Good plan. And if you sell the film rights—which will definitely happen—the film will come out two years from now."

"Precisely."

"And who do you see playing you?"

"Audrey Tautou, who else? Don't you think I look like her?"

"Uh…not particularly."

"Seriously! Our eyes and hair are the same colour!"

"Well, in that case I look like Brad Pitt."

"Two peas in a pod."

"…"

"Uh…when you got here I had the impression you had something to say. Maybe I was wrong…"

"Oh! Yes, I was forgetting…"

"What?"

"Actually, it's not really something to tell you. More like something to give you."

"What did you want to give me?"

"Oh, nothing much. Just $12,000. Less what you owe me for your hideous car, but still a tidy sum."

It wasn't a complicated sentence, but my brain couldn't decode it right away. I am so used to things fizzling out, nothing ever working out well, that my brain circuits controlling reactions to success have long been deactivated. I repeated his last reply dozens of times, trying to understand it, reviewing every possible interpretation. It must have taken me a good two minutes before I came to the conclusion that the literal interpretation was probably the right one. While this mental labour was going on, Sébastien took a piece of paper out of his bag and held it out to me. It was a cheque for $12,000, made out to him, from the Canada Council for the Arts.

"You're kidding me…"

"If I could make such convincing fake cheques, you'd never

catch me eating at Subway."

"It worked…"

"I'd say so."

"We asked for money and they gave it to us… It's crazy."

After I'd gathered myself together, Seb and I arranged to meet the next day at the National Bank, so we could convert this scrap of paper into real money and settle our accounts. For now, I apologized for leaving him so abruptly, but I had to run to tell Jude the news. I called Steve and put his leash on. I was getting ready to leave when Seb called me back.

"Uh…Tess…"

"Yes?"

"Did you know he's a bitch?"

"Hey? What?"

"Steve. He's a she."

"Well, I never!"

"Look."

"Wow. It's true!"

"This is one big day of surprises!"

✖ ··· 29 ··· ✖

CELEBRATIONS

Thinking it would be childish to hold anything back, I launched everything at Jude as soon as I set foot in the apartment. "Steve is a girl and we've got the cash!"

He had the same reaction I did. He stopped what he was doing (the washing up, as it happens) and went to sit in the living room, where he was silent for some time, a perplexed wrinkle striped across his forehead. Then he got up and went to crouch by the dog, who was lapping water from his bowl. "Fuck! You're right! What's the female equivalent of Steve? Sandra? Linda?"

"She's still going to be called Steve, she's used to it. You can't change a dog's name, it might upset them. Caesar said so. And anyway, Steve is fine for a girl: the singer in Fleetwood Mac was called Stevie Nicks."

"Stevie. Not Steve."

"Well, yeah. But I get the feeling you're not focusing on the most important part of my sentence."

"We've got the cash."

"Yes, we've got the cash."

"We sent them an envelope full of bullshit and in return they give us a cheque for twelve thousand bucks. The neighbour was right: and people wonder why the country's in such a mess...

What now?"

"I'm meeting Seb at noon tomorrow: he'll cash the cheque, take his part, and give us the rest. After that, we can start getting ready, pay to renew your licence, buy suitcases and some clothes, etc. But I suggest we begin by celebrating."

"Definitely. But we should still go easy on the celebrating. Remember we're on a tight budget."

"Yes, we'll celebrate sensibly. A nice meal in a real restaurant, that sort of thing, just to mark the event."

The next day, at the appointed time, I met Sébastien outside the National Bank. You often hear it said (especially by poor people) that money can't buy love. Nothing is more wrong. That's all it does buy. People become very affectionate toward you when you spend a lot in their shops or carry out big transactions in their banks. The lady at the counter was kind to the point of obsequiousness while Sébastien was explaining our situation ("I'd like to deposit this cheque into my account and then transfer $6,000 into this young lady's account"), nodding her head and looking at him the way the apostles must have looked at Jesus during his transfiguration. Once the transaction was completed, I rushed to the cash machine to do a balance inquiry. "Available Funds: $6,234.89." I know that doesn't mean much to you, reader—just one single paycheque of yours looks like that—but for me it was an absolute fortune. I went back to Sébastien on the pavement. As we were about to leave, I asked him to wait for me and went into the bank once more to do another balance inquiry. My balance was still up at $6,234.89. This time, I printed it out to show Jude.

Just before we parted ways, at the corner of Eighth, Sébastien said to me, "Um…Tess, I don't want to get involved in things that don't concern me…"

"Oh, don't be shy."

"You said that you and Jude were planning to save to increase your cash. Something tells me you haven't done that…"

"You're right, it didn't work out. We're going to trim our expenses instead."

"All the same, $6,000 is hardly a fortune. You know, I wouldn't mind lending you a bit more money. With even just a thousand bucks extra, things would be a bit less tight…"

"Listen, Sébastien, I might be wrong (in which case you can call me an idiot), but…um…I get the impression that you're only offering because you're afraid you'll never hear from me again now that we're all square."

"What are you talking about? First, we're not all square: you are eternally in my debt for letting you use my name with these institutions."

"Yes, of course, but—"

"I'm kidding."

"Oh."

"But if I understand you correctly, all those times you agreed to have coffee with me were just to spare the feelings of the guy you owed money to."

"Oh, come on! Let's just pretend I didn't say anything."

"Okay, but the offer still stands: a thousand dollars, which you could pay me back in several small instalments when it suits you."

"Well, it would certainly be less tight with an extra thousand bucks. So let's go for it. Once again I don't know how to thank you…"

"I could make some suggestions, but you wouldn't want to hear them."

"You're so crude!"

We returned to the bank. He went in and came out again a few minutes later waving a wad of bills. There was five hundred in hundred-dollar bills, the rest in smaller bills. I stuffed it into the back pocket of my jeans (a month's salary, a hundred hours standing behind containers of cold meat and vegetables wearing an ugly uniform), thanked Sébastien again, and went back home.

I said earlier I'd rather die than be indebted to the neighbour, but I've had to dilute this slightly: we didn't have anyone else handy to look after Steve while we were out celebrating. Since we were only leaving for a few hours, we could just have left her with enough water and food, but she doesn't like being left alone. The one time we tried it, she protested by committing several acts of vandalism (emptying the garbage in Jude's bedroom, disembowelling a cushion, assaulting a tissue, etc.). We got the message. Anyway, we won't be all that indebted to the neighbour: all he has to do is physically be there, which is his speciality. And we're leaving him a fridge full of beer. He'll get drunk playing Xbox and watching smutty videos, and he'll never even notice that he's not in his own house.

At first we thought about reserving a table at Toqué or Laurie Raphaël, or one of those fancy city restaurants, but in keeping with our policy of celebrating sensibly we made do with Le Guéridon in Trois-Rivières. And since we were passing through the regional capital, we decided to combine the useful with the pleasant and take a trip to Les Rivières Mall to make a few purchases for our journey. Some clothes, for starters. Jude wanted nothing to do with buying clothes, but I pointed out that Pennsylvania was a long way away from his mother's washing machine, and that he wouldn't make it very far with his two pairs of jeans, his four moth-eaten T-shirts, his ancient running shoes that cost ten bucks, and the wool sweater he was wearing in his Grade 12 class photo. In any case, he probably wasn't going to be allowed into a top restaurant like Le Guéridon decked out like that. He groused a bit but gave in. I didn't waste this chance: he came out of the mall dressed like a little gentleman. I found him two pairs of shoes at Jack & Jones: a beautiful Santoni pair in leather, and some Nike high-tops. I handed over my debit card without even looking at the total, but just from seeing the love in the sales assistant's eyes I could tell that Jude would be the only person on welfare in the province wearing Santonis. It's pretty simple: you have to pay for quality. Then we got him some pricey underwear from Underwhere? (to encourage businesses who have a stupid play on words as their trading name) and we found the rest in West Coast. As for me, I found happiness in Garage and Jacob Connexion. After that, we went to Bentley and acquired two Skyway sports bags and two Samsonite wheelie suitcases. That would have to do.

We knocked back a few pints at Nord-Ouest, at the corner of Notre-Dame and Forges, and at dusk we ambled over to Le Guéridon. Jude was already wearing his new clothes and his fancy Santoni shoes; as far as I was concerned, I didn't think I needed to change; I was presentable enough in my old clothes. Except then I spilled some Hoegaarden on them, and you can hardly turn up to any restaurant except Stratos Pizza smelling of beer. So we passed by the car, where I picked out an outfit, and then looped back to Rue du Fleuve, thinking we might spot a deserted corner where I could change. I speedily carried out the operation behind the water treatment plant.

"Good, now let's take your old clothes back to the car and go and eat," Jude said.

I said no, we'd wasted enough time already and I was starving to death now, so I ran to chuck everything in the river. Good riddance! After all, I'd had that T-shirt for three or four years, the jeans too; you can hardly say I hadn't made good use of them.

Mr. Fisher reckons the general public is pretty much indifferent to the beauty of words, that most of all they just want to be told a story. I'm not ashamed to admit it: my tastes align pretty well with those of the general public. Words for the sake of it—not really my cup of tea. But I always make an exception for restaurant menus. I, who would prefer to get down on all fours to scrub the floor rather than open a book of poetry, would go to a restaurant just to savour the descriptions of the meals. I can't resist showing you a few examples (taken from Le Guéridon's website, if you want to read the whole thing):

Lightly Steamed Asparagus
with melted Fleur des Monts cheese, Serrano ham, caramelized tomatoes and soft quail egg, summer truffle Banyuls dressing

Creamy Butternut Squash
ribbons of smoked Charlevoix emu and black trumpet mushrooms, walnut and balsamic-glazed walnuts with zabaglione

Turlo Farm 28-Day-Aged Squab
delicately pinked breasts scented with cardamom and confit thighs stuffed with foie gras, smothered in a savoury jus
[This was the main course I had!]

Veal Rice and Wild Prawns
roasted butternut squash gnocchi, buds and leaves of Swiss chard, creamy Samos muscat sauce and morels

Caribou Leg
roasted with Sarawac pepper, pan-fried with wild mushrooms, spiced scarlet pear, pepper sauce with fruits of the forest and Chicoutai butter

La Boutique
rum passionfruit baba, macaroon in a cream puff

```
with strawberry chocolate nectar, lemon cream
cheesecake, served in a delicate glass bowl
```
[This was my dessert!]

```
Cognac
frosted pyramid of crisp sugared almonds,
Romias biscuits, caramelized filberts and maple
butter
```

Pretty, am I right? We let ourselves be guided by euphony as far as wine goes too, ordering a bottle of Vouette et Sorbée Extra-Brut Blanc d'Argile. Later on, a sommelier came over to blather about wine–meal matchmaking. We told him (politely but firmly) to take a hike. For example, with my main course he wanted to have me drink a wine with the banal name of Burgundy Saint-Aubin 2007. I went for a 2003 Fiefs Vendéens, La Grande Pièce, Domaine Saint-Nicolas, and without wanting to cast aspersions on the sommelier, this Fiefs Vendéens and my squabs were as thick as thieves. It was the same with Jude's Magdalen Islands scallops, which were BFFs with his 2006 Lieu-dit Clavin from the Domaine de la Vieille Julienne. And our respective desserts got on so well with the excellent 2001 Autumn Grain sweet Muscat du Pays d'Oc that we couldn't help ordering a second bottle. When Caroline (as our waitress was called) brought us the bill, I went to pay it, taking care to leave it turned over on the tray (what you don't know can't hurt you). Jude asked how I'd worked out the tip without knowing the total of the bill.

"I gave more than not enough... In fact, going by Caro's smile, I gave a lot more than more than not enough."

To be perfectly honest, we were dead drunk when we left Le Guéridon. Going home was unthinkable. Just getting the key into the ignition seemed an impossible task. We could have walked for half an hour toward Trois-Rivières West to find some horrendous motel where we could stay for a few dollars, but we could barely stand up, so we crawled to the Delta. People don't feel especially affectionate toward you when you show up at their hotel stinking of alcohol and asking for the cheapest room (which was still $132!), but with all the love we'd felt that day, we could manage without any from the Delta receptionist. I collapsed on the bed, leaving Jude the task of phoning the neighbour to ask him if he would be so kind as to stay at our place until the next day.

✕···30···✕

TIMING BELT

We got up right before the maid came to tell us that our stay was over. We showered speedily and, after a quick jaunt over to Rue Notre-Dame to make sure the car was still there, we went to Morgane for breakfast (not the one on Notre-Dame, the one on the corner of Royal, to give us a chance to stretch our legs). We felt a bit rough, but less awful than you might have expected after our state the previous evening. We'd got off lightly. After our coffee and brioches, we were as good as new. We took another coffee for the road and went out to get some air. We wandered for a while around the fancy neighbourhoods, but since that label applies to an area of around a hundred square metres in Trois-Rivières, we also wandered round the ugly neighbourhoods. When we hit the river, we retraced our steps and bravely took Sainte-Marguérite up the hill to Cooke Hospital. That brought us to the edge of the university, and, without either of us suggesting it, we somehow ended up sitting outside Gambrinus with two pints of stout. We didn't really even want to: we mostly wanted to convince ourselves that we weren't feeling too morning-after-the-night-before. All the same, we stuck to just the one pint.

When we left Gambrinus, we decided to go back to the car along Des Forges, to change things up. That's how we came to go past Gosselin Photo's window, where the same idea came to us both at the same time: you can't go on holiday without a camera. And if that last sentence seems familiar, it's because I'm coming full circle with my flashback. (Take a few seconds here to be fully dazzled by my impressive command of narrative structure.) I'd never have expected it, but choosing a camera turned out to be as confusing as buying a car. In both cases you take a perverse pleasure in being engulfed in a tidal wave of technical terms, with the barely concealed intention of letting yourself be screwed over. We'd hardly finished saying that we were in the market for a camera when the guy behind the counter started jabbering on about megapixels, shutter speed, lenses, focal length, depth of field, and a whole host of other things. At one point, he interrupted himself to ask us, "By the way, are you looking for an SLR or a point-and-shoot?"

"We just want to take photos. We're going on holiday and we'd like to bring back some memories. We just need a camera that gives a pretty good representation of what you can see when you press the button. We don't want to break the bank either."

A brief flash of disdain passed over his face, as if I'd just confessed to doing it with animals or reading Nora Roberts, but, good salesperson that he was, he rapidly conquered his revulsion and started talking to us about the Canon PowerShot S90, on sale right now. He even (just about) conceded that we were human beings when I waved my debit card under his nose as I announced that I'd take it. We also bought a carrying case and a two-gigabyte memory card, which we managed to fill on the way back to the car. "It takes fucking good pictures, our camera, we didn't get screwed over."

"True. And people bang on about ten megapixels…"

"Yeah, that's a lot of megapixels."

It was right at the Burrill exit in Shawinigan that we first heard the noise, a noise reminiscent of Russian mountain trains going up their first hill, like *tak tak tak tak*, know what I mean? Then it stopped for a moment before starting up again, louder this time, just before the downtown Grand-Mère exit. I could see that the Monte Carlo was struggling (although my foot was on the floor, we were still losing speed), but I was trying not to worry. We've always dealt with our problems like this: ignoring them in the hope that they'll end up resolving themselves. That works about two or three per cent of the time, I'd say. (Like with my debt to the Ministry of Education: in the end they stopped hassling me.) But apparently engine troubles aren't in the category of problems you can wait out. We managed to get to the Irving on the outskirts of the city purely on momentum. "We didn't choose you, but our car just wouldn't go any farther," Jude said, trying to be witty, to the man who came to ask what he could do for us. While two of his henchmen pushed the Monte Carlo inside, we explained what had happened, imitating the noise as best we could. We must have been pretty good because he put forward, on the sole basis of our performance, a provisional diagnosis: "The timing belt must have snapped." He added that we shouldn't have carried on driving after the first *tak tak*; it would have been better to call a tow truck right then and there. He put that in his own words, obviously. We didn't reply, just mumbled, "Yes, sir," and stared at our shoes.

While we waited for the Irving guys to come up with their official diagnosis, we packed our things into our wheelie suitcases and took them home. Steve was wild with joy at seeing us again. She really wanted to give us the cold shoulder to punish us for abandoning her, but she wasn't strong enough. And she forgave and forgot completely when we announced we were going for a walk. The neighbour, who was playing Splinter Cell and drinking beer, asked where we were going so soon. "To the garage. Our timing belt is broken."

"Is it just the timing belt?"

"Well, we don't know yet. We'll know more soon enough."

"I hope for your sake that it's just the timing belt, because if the pump's gone too it's going to cost you an arm and a leg."

"Oh."

On our way to the garage, we made a quick detour to let the dog run around in the hospital grounds. "I wonder what it is?"

"What?"

"A timing belt."

"I guess we'd call it 'une ceinture de synchronisation' in French."

"So what does it synchronize?"

"Search me. Anyway, it's a pain in the ass."

"Sure is, but look on the bright side: if the timing belt was going to snap, better now than during our trip."

"That's true."

"And we can make the most of the car's being at the garage to give it a checkup. Change the oil, pump up the tires, check if anything else is about to break, etc. Then we'll be able to set off without any worries."

"I'm just afraid it's going to cost us a lot. I mean, we did have quite the splurge yesterday…"

"We did, but I forget to tell you: we're richer than you think. Sébastien thought it would be a shame to go with just six thousand bucks, so he lent me an extra thousand. He gave it to me in cash."

"Pretty nice of him! But you didn't leave a big wad of moolah in the apartment when we were out? I don't like to question the neighbour's honesty, but—"

"No, I didn't leave it at home, I was carrying it in the pocket of my…"

"What?"

"Fuck!"

"The pocket of your what?"

"My jeans…"

"Um…not the ones you chucked into the river?"

✖···**31**···✖

ERRATUM

The French for a timing belt isn't "ceinture de synchronisation" but "courroie de transmission." Although timing belts look very ordinary, they are actually extremely rare objects. At least, so I imagine. How else could we explain their exorbitant cost?

✗···32···✗

I don't much like replaying all this, so I'm going to keep it short. We were in the little park on Tenth Avenue, Jude and I sitting on the swings near the bowling green while Steve burned off her excess energy by running aimlessly. She saw a squirrel on the other side of the road, froze for a second with her ears pricked, and then she was off like a shot. We yelled her name, but apparently her predator instinct had got the upper hand; she didn't even slow down. To be completely honest, I don't think the truck was much over the speed limit. Seventy or seventy-five in a fifty zone, pretty standard. Basic courtesy should have led him to stop after he ran over our dog, but maybe he didn't have time, maybe it was a question of life or death, maybe he was driving a badly injured person, or his wife was going to give birth, who knows. In any case, it doesn't count as a hit and run when it's a dog.

We stayed frozen idiotically on the swings for a good minute before we raced toward the road (even for problems that have zero chance of resolving themselves, we can't help testing it). She was lying on her side, breathing rapidly. Her eyes were open wide but she didn't seem to see us. If the man who lives across from the park hadn't come out of his house and helped us to get her to the vet in the back of his pickup, we'd probably have stayed there, totally stunned, until she died. We were spaced out, horrified in a way we'd rarely experienced, and as ineffectual as always. When we came out of our torpor, we were in an office and some lady in a white coat was listing all the injuries Steve had suffered, some ribs broken, others cracked, two fractures in her left hind leg and one in her pelvis. "Can she be fixed, madam?" (She must have been five years younger than me, but what with her white coat and the diplomas on the walls, the "madam" seemed obligatory.)

"Yes, we can operate, and if everything goes well she'll come through it without any serious consequences. Maybe a slight limp. I'll give you a few minutes to discuss it."

"Why would we need to discuss it?"

"Well, it's a pretty expensive operation."

"How much?"

"Eight hundred dollars, assuming there aren't any complications. Call it a thousand with taxes and overnights. That's not including medication."

"Yeah…but we don't really have a choice. We could hardly operate on her ourselves, could we, madam?"

She operated on Steve the same day and kept her in for observation for forty-eight hours in a big cage that she shared (albeit with a grille between them) with an extremely anxious pug who'd swallowed a bunch of keys. At first, she seemed too woozy to even notice we were there, but on the second day she thumped her tail on the ground when she heard our voices. When it was all over we went to pick her up. The vet certainly seemed pleased with her work. She strongly advised us to not let our animal do any intense exercise for the first week, not even walks, but just put out some newspaper on the balcony for her to do her business on, make sure she took her medications, etc. Once we were home, we settled her on the cushion we'd bought for her the day she arrived (and which she had always scorned, but now she was too weak to protest), and treacherously concealed in her food a dose of the medicine for which we'd just paid through the nose at the clinic, and we left her to sleep. We'd done our part—it was up to nature to do the rest. It was only then that we felt the stress fall away, leaving an enormous weariness. Jude collapsed onto the couch, swearing and letting out a great sigh. I went to the kitchen to get us some beers, but we didn't have a single one left. I stood in front of the fridge for a few moments, wondering if I had the strength to go out and buy some. Then I remembered that we were nearly out of TP and I was going to have to go out anyway, so I might as well get it over with now. Once at the convenience store, I realized I was starving (we hadn't eaten much the last few days). On top of the two-four of beer and the TP, I picked up a whole bunch of crap—Party Mix, popcorn, jerky, cheese strings, etc. I handed my card to the cashier.

"Oops! It's not working…"

"What's not working?"

"It says insufficient funds."

"No, that's impossible, try again."

"Hmmm… No, it's saying the same thing again."

"Uh…okay, maybe I've got cash."

I had a few dozen dollars in my wallet. I was a bit short, so I had to put the TP back. Once I got back to the house, I made us a snack and opened us each a beer. We drank and ate in silence. Steve was sleeping soundly at our feet, knocked out by painkillers. At one point she woke up, and Jude seized the moment to give her a lecture: "I hope that's put you off hunting squirrels for a while, you great fool! If you ever do such a stupid thing again, I don't know what we'll do to you…" She listened to Jude's speech all the way through, more out of politeness than anything else, then her head dropped and she went back to sleep. The threat made no difference to her; she didn't seem overly worried by what we might do to her. I think she was starting to figure us out: she knows we'll never do anything.

ACKNOWLEDGEMENTS

Thank you to Christopher Dummitt,
François Blais, Hazel Millar, Jay MillAr,
Stuart Ross and Pablo Strauss.

—J.S.

ABOUT THE AUTHOR

Idra Labrie/Perspective

FRANÇOIS BLAIS is one of the most exciting contemporary voices of Quebec literature. Considered an underground superhero of French writing, he is the author of 9 novels and a collection of short stories. *Document 1*, which was released in French in 2013 to great critical acclaim, is his first novel to be translated into English.

■ ■ ■

JC SUTCLIFFE is a writer, translator, book reviewer, and editor. She has lived in England, France, and Canada.

COLOPHON

Manufactured as the first English edition of *Document 1*
in the spring of 2018 by Book*hug.

Distributed in Canada by the Literary Press Group: lpg.ca

Distributed in the United States by Small Press Distribution:
spdbooks.org

Shop online at bookthug.ca

BOOK
PRODUCTION
WAR ECONOMY
STANDARD

Type + design by Tree Abraham
Copy edited by Stuart Ross